You Made Me Kill You

By Allison Relyea

Fiction:

You Made Me Kill You

A Cure Through Love

Poetic Self-Help:

Undoing Unearthing Becoming

The Honeymoon of Healing

medicine

This is a work of fiction. All names, characters, and incidents are based on the author's imagination, or are used fictitiously. Any depiction to real incidences or persons is entirely coincidental. This is not based on a true story.

Cover design by Rhys Davies (www.rhysspieces.com)
ISBN: 979-8-9886009-3-0

For the hurt souls who use writing as a means to escape, to feel, and who are brave enough to share it

You Made Me Kill You

A Suspense Novel

Allison Relyea

I have just about eight rocks comfortably tucked into the pockets of my sundress. It's not all black, like the kind of dress you would typically find on a New York woman. It's a very pale yellow, not quite pastel. A soft crème, really. Small sunflowers with tiny red buds in the middle bleed through from top to bottom. The dress hangs loose, nearly down to my ankles, which are covered by heavy leather boots. I would have said chunky, but that word disgusts me. *Chunky, moist, and flow*: three words that should be struck from the dictionary.

Anyway, back to the rocks. There are four in each pocket, each nearly palm-size. Some are wet—a soft gray, with dark patches from the moisture—and some are dry. They are heavy, some of their surfaces fuzzy, like thick dust coating a smooth surface, and some feel rigid.

The rocks weigh me down, pulling on the dress and causing it to hang low on me. *The point of the rocks.*

But I did not put them there. *Another point of the rocks.*

November 11th, 2022

LOCAL WOMAN FOUND IN EAST RIVER POLICE SUSPECT SUICIDE

NEW YORK, NY – At approximately 6:45 this morning, two young women jogging along the east river discovered what "looked like a body" floating just off of Pier 35 on the Lower East Side, below the FDR Drive. They immediately called local law enforcement.

NYPD Boat Patrolmen were able to recover the body. Police "found no signs of foul play" and ruled it a suicide.

The NYPD is asking for the public's help in identifying the deceased. She is Caucasian, between forty and forty-five, with no tattoos, piercings, or identifying marks. If you have any information that might help the case, the NYPD urges you to come forward.

PART ONE

CHAPTER ONE
DIANA

The decision to kill your husband is not an easy one. I would know. I have spent the last decade making it.

None of the stages are easy: not the abuse that leads to the decision, the decision itself, or the aftermath of the decision. Certainly not his death.

I still loved him, *them*, after all.

It is humiliating, facing the reality of the man you married. Whether or not a person (a victim … survivor … however one wants to deem oneself) is mentally fit—whether she blames herself or not—the whole thing is embarrassing. To think that the person you married … saw a future with, made love to, wanted children with, if even for a split second … slept in the same bed with, laughed with, connected with … could rape, hit, punch, kick, stomp, choke you.

It is incredibly shameful.

At least for me.

And I do not like to be embarrassed.

The reality is, the decision to kill your husband can come to fruition fairly quickly.

My first beat me so badly, I couldn't leave the house for weeks at a time. Sometimes, my eyes would swell too tight to open. Other times, I was literally unable to walk, or there were just too many cuts and scratches on my face for me to be seen. Any of this would have raised serious concerns with anyone I interacted with, whether I knew them personally or not, so I was house-bound until I healed.

My second husband molested children, boys and girls—"They look the same at that age," he said after I caught video footage he had. "It isn't cheating," he also tried justifying. He was a second-grade teacher, and to think he was entrusted with children in such a fashion actually made me vomit. So, I had to kill him.

My third also beat me. Raped me, too.

I had to wonder if I was some sort of walking target.

And that brings me to my fourth and current husband, James, a cheating and lying bastard.

Okay, maybe that isn't enough grounds for murder, but at this point, I have done it enough times to have learned that the thrill is what attracts me to these men, and it entices me. Like a Dexter Morgan. We could have been partners in crime.

My name is Eden Lowell. Pronounced Lo-vell. I have been married to James Lowell for almost three years, the shortest duration of all four of my unions.

But we have now reached my favorite part of marriage: planning the murder.

You might be wondering how it is that I have not been caught. No, I do not have a kill room, nor do I dump their bodies in the ocean, like Dexter. I make them look like tragic accidents: car wrecks, falls, suicides.

James is an airline pilot. I should have known he would cheat. Flying to and from cities like Paris, Milan, Berlin, etc., where the women are exceptionally beautiful. How could I have been so stupid?

Or maybe I wasn't.

Maybe I subconsciously knew, and chose it.

So I could kill.

I look down at my notes.

Eden is malevolent. She has no empathy ... detached from reality. It's as though she is looking through a glass window when she watches people—both young and old—express emotion. I have the word psychopath circled three times. *Her shrew, cunning personality is what men find so attractive.*

Maybe she'll be in cahoots with the other woman, the mistress? Maybe they conspire to kill him together. Take his money? Plan to scam other men?

It's the informative stuff, part of the outline, and not very interesting, I know, but I feel stuck. I gloss over it a few times to try and feel out the characters more.

I'm not Eden, I should point out.

My name is Diana Steinbeck, and I'm a writer from New York City.

Not a murderer.

After an exciting, but repetitive, decade in journalism, I toyed with being a novelist. My last piece as a journalist covered the story of a man who set his ex-wife's house on fire. He meant only to scare her, but killed her and their son in the process. Their bodies were found amongst the charred rubble. My piece on the "Fire Father" (as he was dubbed), is lost amongst the hundreds of published and unpublished pieces on my external hard drive. I didn't finish the story. I couldn't. That was the day I walked out on my job as a journalist, and I haven't looked back since.

I turned that abrupt departure into an opportunity to write a novel. I found it more fulfilling, invigorating, and creative. I still do.

My first book is a collection of personal essays, in the genres of self-help and women's interests, with an occasional op-ed. My second, a romance novel, follows a young couple from America to a small town in Italy after they inherit a coffee shop from a relative the husband didn't know he had. It is loosely based on a dream my husband and I had of moving to a small town in Italy or Switzerland or Malta. We had a lot of dreams, actually. A lot of griefs, too, most of which began as dreams. And yet, a decade later, we are still in New York City. Not that there is anything wrong with the city. I love Manhattan.

Although both books sold mediocrely, they provided me with a steady income. I was grateful, and I quickly fell in love with this new area of my field.

The Convent, my third, is my most successful piece. It was so well-received, in fact, it was an international bestseller with over ten million copies sold in over a dozen languages. The protagonist, Jillian, seeks refuge in a convent, disguising herself as a nun to escape her abusive husband.

My fourth, *Mathilde*, is also a dark thriller. It is a fictionalized story of Emile Sagee's disturbing life. In the 1800s, Sagee was a schoolteacher who was haunted by a doppelganger appearing as a ghostly figure. She was fired from several schools because this ghoul/spirit appeared in the corner of the classroom while she was at the blackboard, or roamed the hallways when she was elsewhere. The twist: everyone but Sagee could see the figure. That book sold five million copies worldwide.

Mathilde was published less than two years after *The Convent* … which was almost three years ago now. That is part of why I am eager to begin writing the next one—the one with the terrible, informative outline I'm currently staring at, wondering where my creative pull has gone.

It is called *The Wife I Should Be*, which is a play on the main character's thirst for murder. She relinquishes that urge through the slayings of her multiple husbands who, in her mind, deserve it. In her mind, she's doing a public service by ridding the world of them.

The book is in its early stages as I consider the twist. Perhaps she and James's mistress, Lola, plan to kill him together. As a pilot, he makes good money, but it is his family money that would be enough for Eden and Lola to split. *And then maybe Eden and Lola turn on one another.*

I try not to be too decisive about the ending just yet. Sometimes, as the nature of the book progresses, new ideas come, and things change. I outline a few different plausible endings, and as the book develops, the best-fitting puzzle pieces reveal themselves to me.

I am often asked how and where I find the inspiration for such dark plots, and honestly, I hate that question. Dark and thrilling is all I know. I think it has something to do with the works and films I devoured a child: *A Time to Kill*, *Blue Velvet*, *The Shining*, *Rosemary's Baby*. My parents were not neglectful, *per se*, but I liked to enter a world darker than my own, lonelier than my own. I am comforted by characters saving themselves or their children. So, it is only natural that my two bestsellers are of that category.

My storylines come to me at random times and places. I never have to search for them. Thank God—or whatever is "up" there, because I don't know if there is a God—for that. I could be jogging, in a doctor's office, in bed, cooking eggs, in the middle of sex, or cycling, and a brilliant idea I absolutely must jot down manifests itself in my brain. Sometimes, if I'm not in a position to take notes, I am forced to continuously replay it in my head, so I won't forget the details.

Writing, and the worlds we have built inside of it, is a mirror to the subconscious. And during the three years I haven't been writing, I have been grieving.

I am anxious about how *The Wife I Should Be* will sell. What if my hiatus has left me dead in the pool of new authors and books? What if it does even less than *Mathilde*?

Sam, my agent, urges me to "just focus on the writing," not the numbers. That's like when my friends told me to focus on my marriage when my daughter was stillborn. To do so isn't just hard. It feels impossible.

I have made enough to live more than comfortably—and in

Manhattan!—but my writing is the only aspect of my life that I have control over creating, growing, and completing. I escape my shitty reality and invade someone else's.

I don't need a psychologist to tell me this is the result of my infertility, my failed attempts at becoming a mother. My way to find control.

I set aside my growing outline and begin preparing for my consultation with psychologist Maureen Sinclair. I must admit I love her name: *Maureen Sinclair.* So fancy and elegant. *Sinclair.* Saying it out loud feels like liquid velvet on the tongue.

Now a practicing therapist, for many years she specialized and worked in the field of psychopaths, what I am considering writing Eden as. Investigative journalism is not lost on me. I still prefer intimate, face-to-face contact in terms of research, and when I begin a novel, I start by outlining the research I need to do in order to develop the plot. I can't outline what I don't know. I need more than Google searches, which lead me down a rabbit hole of psychology-based medical journals, websites, articles, and more. A great resource, of course, the internet, but it won't respond when I am curious or conflicted.

I am blessed to have escaped growing up in the age of social media and digital resources, depending on a computer for socialization, information, and entertainment.

I open my laptop and return to Dr. Maureen Sinclair's business profile. Not only do I take my own work seriously, but the field in which I am writing, too. Credibility is the key to a writing a good, well-rounded novel.

I review her specialties: addiction, anxiety, bipolar disorder, emotional disturbance, and narcissistic personality. She lists her extensive experience in psychopathy and dissociative identity disorder—or, the long-debated "multiple personality" diagnosis (which intrigues me so much, it might just be the subject matter of my next book). She has written numerous articles and has over two dozen presentations about psychopaths under her belt. In other words, her work and knowledge are perfect, convenient tools for my research.

I look over my office, which is, like the entire apartment, quiet. There's a slight chill in the air; autumn is coming. In New York City, that brings maybe a handful of comfortable days before it dips into freezing temperatures. I grab the sweater that has been sitting in the corner of my office for who knows how long and drape it over myself.

Miller is due home soon, but it doesn't feel like a homecoming. When you lose everything, you tend to lose *everything*. Especially the people around you. Still, he is the only tangible thing I have left, and I do still love him. Though some days, I'm not sure he feels the same.

I push the thoughts of him out of my head, click out of Dr. Sinclair's website, and shut my computer down for the evening, aware of the unease feeling that sets in my stomach.

CHAPTER TWO
DIANA

Following my brief consultation with Dr. Maureen Sinclair, our one o'clock appointment the following Thursday comes fairly quickly.

It is early September, a settled time in the city; people are back from their summer vacations at the Hamptons or Jersey Shore and comfortably settled back into their routines. The city is crowded again, which I prefer to the vacant summer streets. Dr. Sinclair's office is two blocks from Washington Square Park; I always enjoy walking beneath the arch, with a perfect view of the Empire State Building. The park is crowded, bustling with NYU students, men playing checkers and chess, and entertainers in the dry fountain performing a show for what looks like a dozen or so people.

Dr. Sinclair's office is on the third floor. It's comfortably small, a cozy corner room with a view of West 7th Street. I can't help but people-watch from the window: a coffee shop from which patrons walk in and out, a bank, laundry mat; joggers, groups friends, children, solo businesswomen and men walking up and down the street.

Her office is minimally decorated but crowded with furniture. Two identical black ladder bookcases are filled with relics and books. I catch a few titles: *The Developing Mind, The Gift of Therapy*, *Principles of Psychology*. There are empty vases in various light tones of green and crème. Between the bookcases is a spacious black desk with drawers on each side, gold knobs, and sharp, carved legs. I love desks and all their unique details. I imagine myself writing at them, wondering what kinds of books might be born from them. I am a different writer depending on the setting. What I create at the Starbucks in Union Square is different from what I create on an airplane, in a car, in my apartment, or on a park bench.

Despite my attempt to disengage my eyes from her desk, Dr. Sinclair sits adjacent to it, so I can't help but note the stacks of papers, two bottles of water, paper cup with a stain at the top (which I assume is tea, given that she is English—stereotypical, I know) covering its surface. Her black purse hangs against the stiff, wooden chair in front of it.

Dr. Sinclair is in a teddy-bear brown, velvet, padded armchair with a high back. It looks comfortably deep. A black side table is adjacent to her, and her phone is face down on it beside a water tumbler and two small notepads.

Across from her, I am sitting on a matching brown, three-seated couch with a pillow on each end. Two square, marble-topped tables are also opposite me, on top of which are identical lamps and tissues perfectly symmetrical. I scoff—*tissues*?

A geometric-patterned rug covers most of the floor, and two floral art prints hang on the wall adjacent to the door. The rest of the walls are comfortably bare, painted a soft, pastel, rosy pink.

Dr. Sinclair drums her finger on the side of her chair and touches her top lip to her nose. She looks inquisitive.

It is our first session of me researching my character Eden, and *role-playing* as Eden. I had a feeling she was skittish, unsure about the proposal. "Thank you again for helping me with my research," I say, grateful she accepted.

She nods with a smile. Dr. Sinclair is a bit plump—curvaceous—but not overweight. Despite the narrowness of her face, it appears round and full. *Squishy*, I dare say. On someone else, it might look cute. She has a small mole to the left of her nose and green eyes that, though they appear bright in color, look tired and sad.

Then again, so do mine.

Our eyes are mirrors to the saddest things we have seen—

the things that never leave us. They reflect out through our eyes. I wonder about the secrets behind hers: the events and people projecting from them into mine. I look away, afraid if I stare too long, she will be able to see my secrets.

Her dingy, thin, chestnut hair is styled in a bob. I spot a few strands of gray, though it could be the lighting. I also notice wrinkles in the skin of her chest. I internally smile. Her hands are steady, and there is a gold band on her ring finger.

Since one of my requests is to be profiled as my character—to come into some of our sessions *as* Eden—I decide to begin there.

"So, I was thinking," I begin. "I could give you a brief outline of my book. Or, if you would prefer not to know much beforehand and treat this as a traditional therapy session for Eden, we can start that way?"

"You can start wherever feels comfortable for you," she answers. "Knowing a patient's history is certainly beneficial to the work—patterns can often suggest future behavior. How you want to introduce that is up to you."

So ... what then? "My knowledge of psychopaths is limited, as is my knowledge on the psychology of serial killers. I know it's a little *Law & Order*ish, but being accurate is important to me. It's important to me to tell the truth. Perhaps we could run through that, and in our next session, I can come in as Eden."

"Sounds like a plan."

As she begins, I immediately notice how she talks about psychopathy like it is unique to her. She speaks not just with fascination, but enthusiasm—emphasizing certain words, using her hands, and leaning forward in her chair. Like it is hers to own.

"What really denotes a psychopath is their lack of empathy and remorse," she says. "They don't recognize emotions in themselves or in others. They have no way of understanding, on an interpersonal level, another's experience. That, of course, makes the dangerous ones *really* dangerous. The non-dangerous ones are …"

"Assholes?"

"Stubborn."

Now I feel like the asshole. "I'm sorry." I change the subject. "Eden is married. Is that odd?"

"Psychopaths don't usually know they're psychopaths," Dr. Sinclair explains. "Most are high functioning. They are not all murderous, as they're often portrayed. One neuroscientist did a scan of his own brain and found out *he* is a psychopath. His name is James H. Fallon, not to be confused with Jimmy Fallon, if you want to read up on him.

"I'm torn." Dr. Sinclair pauses, puts a pen to her lip, and tilts her head as her eyes scale me up and down. "The word *psychopath*, and other terms like narcissist, bi-polar, borderline personality disorder, dissociative identity disorder—or multiple personality, as people refer to it—are improperly used in today's society. Suddenly, everyone's ex is a narcissist; a girl and her new boyfriend are codependent, and if you experience depression and happiness simultaneously, you're bipolar. The criteria are much deeper."

She elaborates in detail on the neurological explanations and a psychopath's limitations: the pre-frontal cortex, the part of the brain responsible for cognitive control and impulsivity; the orbitofrontal cortex, decision-making and learning from experiences; and lastly, the amygdala, which processes emotions and internal and external threats. "A psychopath trying to comprehend another person's emotions is like trying to see out of your elbow: we can envision what that would look like, but we don't waste our days trying to figure out the how. So, we don't care. Don't think about it."

I nod as I scribble down notes.

"Psychopaths are entirely superficial. They may take jobs in high positions to feel superior and dominating. They get off on harassment, humiliating people, and power. They are highly manipulative, which is what makes some of them challenging subjects or patients, *if* they enter into therapy."

I raise my hand, almost like a student in class, and she pauses. "Would you even want them to come to therapy? I mean, you can't *grow* a conscience. In a perfect world, how would you positively treat them? How would you like to see them function? Can you truly exist in the world without feeling co-mpassion, empathy, cravings?"

"I would like to see therapy improve their negative react-ions … for them to recognize that their actions have conse-quences."

"But if they don't fear the consequences, do they really matter?"

"I would educate them on *why* they matter. There's a void in the psychopathic brain, which can make for a boring sub-ject, when non-violent. But having him acknowledge how it affects his life and learning coping skills and habits to manage violent behaviors and control substance abuse can be very eff-ective."

I want to say *they won't care why consequences matter,* but I stop myself. They are not wolves; they are people. And I don't want Dr. Sinclair to think I am challenging her. She pa-uses my thoughts when she continues to speak about their ch-aracteristics like a walking textbook.

"They are meticulous and cunning. And they are born this way. It's rare to develop into a psychopath, like as a result of trauma, but it's not impossible. Every single psychopath I ha-ve encountered has had a traumatic background of some sort. I have only met one individual who came from a loving, well-rounded family and environment."

"So, you believe in nurture over nature?"

"I ... believe both are to be considered; it depends on the subject. What is Eden's background?"

I feel my cheeks flush and my eyes widen. I hope to avoid choking on my words as I begin. "Not a great one. No father, mother addicted to drugs. She dropped out of high school and moved in with her much older boyfriend—her first murder victim—when she was sixteen. He abused and raped her. I thought having a female psychopathic serial killer would be a unique angle."

"It certainly is. Female psychopaths are much scarcer. They also have different characteristics than males. Male psychopaths focus their control on environment; females focus on manipulating relationships through deceit, lies, and promiscuity. They're also less likely to be homicidal—their rage is focused inward, whereas men express it outwardly."

I feel embarrassed; I did not know that, and I think she senses it.

"But you shouldn't be discouraged. A female psychopath may kill under the right circumstances ... like if they feel repeatedly humiliated, out of control, tricked, or abused. They have a talent for reading people, identifying their weak points, and exploiting a personal vendetta. Psychopaths don't change. They don't feel a need to. Male or female, they are not in control of their urges, so they may not hesitate to kill a spouse who has been beating or raping them, for example. I've seen it myself, with a young man. His mother had been making him touch her for years before inviting her female friends to have sex with him. When he was older, he went on a killing spree, murdering them all. This was in California. It was a unique case. A psychopath abused as a child who grew up to be a serial killer."

"It makes sense."

"What does?" she asks, tilting her head slightly.

"Why he killed them."

"Why is that?"

"His mom and friends raped him."

"It's an unimaginable experience … one that kept me up at night. But I don't condone what he did."

"Neither do I. But you can understand why, can't you?"

Dr. Sinclair licked her lips. "Yes. I suppose I can."

***

Settled back in my office at home, I feel even more awkward as I reconstruct my notes from my session with Dr. Sinclair than I did while sitting across from her.

I was really off my game, which is unlike me. I was also apprehensive about sharing my work … also unlike me. I'm usually poised and trusting.

Dr. Sinclair is not the first psychologist I have consulted with for a novel. When I was writing *The Convent*, I was graciously invited to attend several group therapy sessions for domestic violence and abuse survivors. Each participant signed consent waivers, and I never even took notes. I simply listened to understand—to feel—their experiences. I think they were grateful just to be heard. Some even expressed gratitude: "Thank you for wanting to tell our stories."

I worked closely with that particular therapist to gain an accurate and raw understanding of what my character would go through: the initial abuse, rationalization, and self-blame. I came to understand why a survivor might not leave the abuser, and the strength it takes to do so. I considered the psychology of both the victim and the abuser—words I didn't care to use, but found applicable and necessary at the time.

But with Dr. Sinclair, there is a light cast on *me* … a new way to be seen.

CHAPTER THREE DIANA

I am still in my office when Miller gets home. I don't go out to greet him. Not for any particular reason. It has been years since I have, and I hardly see how it would matter now.

Though I spend most of my time working from different locations, it's nice to have an office at home, especially during the winter season, complete with blizzards and below-freezing temperatures. The small den just off our bedroom more than suffices. Originally, it was to be a nursery, but I have done everything in my power to make it the polar opposite of that.

Of course, my desk is the most important piece in my office. It is long, double-tiered, light-oak, contemporary—an extravagant purchase of five thousand dollars, but one I was proud to make with the earnings from the sale of my first book (along with this apartment). White shelves with books and plants hang above it, beside framed photos of the covers of my books and some of my favorite reviews from *The New York Times*. A large Monstera plant (colloquially known as the Swiss cheese plant) grows in the corner next to my filing cabinets. Since I am old-fashioned when it comes to writing, I store the physical, hand-written copies of my writing in cabinets for superstitious reasons. Laptops are too easily prone to break down.

As are people, I suppose.

In the corner behind my desk, next to a large vertical window, is a beautiful rocking chair. I bought it when I was pregnant; I spent so many hours rocking back and forth, rubbing my belly and feeling my baby girl moving around. I didn't want to sell it along with the rest of the baby furniture. I had already built a memory with it. The only other material representation of that time of my life still sits on the top shelf of the closet by the door—a basket of unworn infant clothes Miller and I bought in different countries, scented only by grief. I choose not to think about it. I choose not to think about a lot of things.

Beside the rocking chair are two bookshelves nailed to the wall holding my own books and some of my all-time favorites: *1984*, *The Bell Jar, East of Eden, Letters to Milena, Jane Eyre,* and *Wuthering Heights.*

I slip into my slippers and walk to the shelf, removing the Brontë sister's books. I had read quotes—like, "I have little left in myself—I must have you. The world may laugh—may call me absurd, selfish—but it does not signify. My very soul demands you: it will be satisfied, or it will take deadly vengeance on its frame," and "He's more myself than I am. Whatever our souls are made of, his and mine are the same," —to Miller so often it was like they were written for us. I have so many pages tabbed and quotes underlined, it is like a museum of our lost words … of our founded love.

"Di?" Miller calls from the other room.

I jerk slightly from my knees, and I had forgotten he was home, and put the books back in order: Charlotte Brontë first, Emily second. "In the office!" I shout, as I sit back at my desk.

His footsteps approach and eventually, I hear him say, "I'm home."

I turn myself in my swivel chair. "Yeah. I see that." I don't mean to sound unwelcoming or cold. I just don't know what else to say. I can't seem to find my words lately, which is frustrating. As a writer, I should have an endless supply of them. Still, even I'm stumped when I play Wordle.

Miller half-smiles at me, and I half-smile back.

We are playing our roles: *I'm okay. He's okay. We're okay.*

When he leans his head against the door and removes his jacket, I think, *God, he's sexy.* He has a debonair look to him: clean-shaven, slender-jawed, perfectly shaped eyebrows that hardly require maintenance (you can imagine his excitement when I pluck a few long strands), glossy honey-brown eyes, and dark-brown hair. He works out at the gym a few times a week before or after work, but he is also blessed with a naturally strong physique. He doesn't have a gut or beer belly; sometimes, a little pouch in the cold months. He has pale, very clear skin, almost ceramic-like. He has hardly any moles, except for a little one on his butt I used to love, and a single scar on the top of his forehead resulting from a tumble out of his child seat when he hit his head on the corner of the dinner table, requiring a few stitches.

Miller is still smiling, and in that moment, I *want* him. But I stop myself, as I always do. For us, sex is a reminder of what cannot come from it. So, I turn away.

"You've been in here a lot lately," he whispers.

And he has been out a lot lately.

"I told you, I've been working on a new manuscript."

His smile becomes wider. "I'm glad to see you getting back into the swing of things … more like your old self. What's it about?"

I want to say there isn't an "old" self or a "new" self … that there is just *my*self. And I don't believe I will ever be the perfectly happy and fun-spirted woman I once was. I also hate the term "swing of things." It's like he's saying he didn't like when I laid in bed, depressed, barely eating, barely showering … not that anyone would, but it would be nice if he could understand how difficult it's all been for me. Of course, I choose not to say this to avoid the inevitable result. I bite the inside of my bottom lip to fight the urge.

"I'm still working on developing it," I say. In the past, I told him about all of my books in their beginning stages. Even the ones that never became anything. And he has supported me in all ways. He listened while I bounced ideas off of him, read outlines, sent me articles about related topics; it does make me sad that we have lost that. But I'm hoping the work I'm doing, both in this novel and outside of it, will help us find each other again.

I inhale deeply and realize how empty my stomach is. I haven't eaten all day. "I'll tell you when I'm further along. How was your day?" My tone is about as flat and dull as our conversation.

"A couple of kids wrote penis on the girl's bathroom door."

I roll my eyes and chuckle.

"To be young, right?"

I lean my arm on my desk and nod, though I would never want to be that young again. Thirty, maybe, but not thirteen.

Miller is a middle-school principal on the Lower East Side—the youngest in the city at the time of his hiring. He's very smart, an intellect; he enjoys reading classics like Kafka and Baldwin, speaks Spanish and Italian, and educating himself on as many topics as he can.

"I was going to order Chinese for dinner," I say. "I haven't made it to the grocery store." I lean back into my chair and bite my pen. "Or do you want to go to Chinatown? Maybe walk around a little?" I pull my legs up on the chair, rest my chin on my knees, and smile.

He shakes his head. "Nah, let's order in."

He leans in to kiss me, which feels very misleading. I am not surprised he doesn't want to go out. We rarely do. We live together, but apart. Sometimes, I think he stays with me out of pity, like I am an invalid, and it enrages me.

Then again, I sometimes wonder … *am I*?

Dinner is quiet, as usual. We try not to eat on our eleven-thousand-dollar couch, so instead, we sit on the carpet below, our backs to it. It might seem contrary, considering we have a dining room table just to the left, between the kitchen and living room, but we do what we can to avoid emotional intimacy. When we finish, we migrate to the couch, and Miller turns on the sports network as I flick through my phone. Our cats, Lucy and Ethel, purr on my lap and stare at me with begging eyes. A second dinner won't kill them; I walk over and give them a handful of leftovers.

Miller and I flirt a little in the bathroom while we brush our teeth, and when the lights are off, Lucy and Ethel snoring at the foot of the bed, Miller slides close to me and sighs deeply—invitingly.

I don't respond.

He does it again.

I know what he wants, but I can't give it to him.

He knows it, too, which is why he doesn't ask or press me about it, but he shifts his body a few times, so I feel guilty.

I can't sleep now. My thoughts are a mess of how little sex we have had in the past year, how little intimacy we have shared in the past few years, and how unhappy we have been over the last decade. Even if the sex returns, the emotion, intimacy, and passion don't.

"Di?" he whispers.

I want to burst into tears and tell him I *want* to have sex with him—to fuck me over and over until we're back in love—but I can't. "Yeah?"

He sighs, disappointed at the crack in my voice.

"I'm sorry."

He kisses my cheek. "You don't have to be sorry. I just wish you'd stop punishing yourself. Or at least *want* to have sex with me."

"I … do," I admit, my voice barely above a whisper.

He leans in and kisses me again. He lowers his lips, kisses my neck, and groans softly. "Then let's try."

He's still kissing my neck, softly sucking on it, as I feel the stirrings of longing and reach for his hand, placing it onto my breast. For a moment, I like it. "Okay," I say.

I turn over, and we are face to face with the comfort of our blanket over us. I don't like my body being fully seen, even in the dark. I slide in closer to him, so we are skin to skin against each other. I love being this way, against him, feeling the beat of his heart against mine, breathing in his natural scent and a bit of mint from his toothpaste.

The mattress sinks in beneath me as he sits up and presses his lips against mine. He positions himself over me, the covers pulling up, and places his hands against my hips. He kisses my chest and slowly makes his way between my breasts, cupping one in his hand, and moves down between my thighs. "You can relax, baby. I'll go slow," he says.

I try to, as my legs are stiff with anxiety. He puts his mouth between them. I fake an orgasm, to get it over with fast, and he pulls the covers from out around him and puts himself inside of me. He leans over my body, whispering in my ear, but I am too anxious to speak.

It feels *okay*, but something isn't right.

A tear runs down my cheek, a slight tickle. He leans up again and puts his hand on my belly; uncontrollably, I lose it. I start screaming for him to get off of me. It's a reflex, and I instantly regret it.

"Jesus Christ, Di." He takes himself out of me. He hasn't finished, and I feel guilty.

He gets out of the bed, nearly pulling the covers with him, but I grab them, so they don't fall.

"I'm sorry, Mil, I …" The tears stream down my cheeks.

"Just stop … stop it."

The light of the bathroom illuminates the room, and I notice how beautiful our bed looks for a moment. The creases in the sheets where his body was and the dent in his pillow. I can smell him. And he's my favorite smell.

I continue to cry as he closes the bathroom door, everything dark besides the sliver of light emanating out from the crack above the floor. I put my hand on the empty sheets beside me and fall asleep, regret still spilling from my eyes, not knowing when he will return to bed.

Or if he will.

CHAPTER FOUR
DIANA

Today, I am Eden.

It is a lie, of course—a lie approved by Dr. Sinclair.

I wonder, *is a lie still a lie if another person is privy to it? What constitutes a lie?*

I considered bringing a tape recorder—how ancient of me, considering the voice note feature on my phone—but I am uncomfortable recording without Dr. Sinclair's permission and worry she would be inauthentic if she consented.

I spent the days leading up to this session imagining how Eden would talk and feel, writing up a character description, an outline of her life, and ultimately, a description of what drove her to be a malice murderer. That was clever: *malice murderer.*

Malice Murderer sounds more appealing than *The Wife I Should Be*, but upon further contemplation, I decide it's too vague. We don't like to admit it, but we do judge books by their covers. As if that is a bad thing, to judge something based on a first appearance. Sometimes, that is all we have to go on. You cannot make a first impression more than once. It is either good, or it is not. Besides, I don't love the word "malice."

Sometimes, I hate how a writer's mind wanders off, but that is the price we pay for our creativity. There is seldom a time when a thought that runs through my mind does not make it into a piece, give me an idea for another piece, or become the foundation of a new piece.

Malice Murderer is out. But Dr. Sinclair is in.

I jump right into it: "I suspect my husband is cheating on me. I'm angry, and I want revenge."

"What gives you that feeling?"

"He's a pilot, and he's fucking sexy; *has the dick of a God.*" I pause, uncomfortable with my forward and detailed description, but then continue. "He knows he can attract any woman, so … who wouldn't want to fuck him? Plus, you've heard about airline pilots, I'm sure." I don't mean to, but I smirk.

"Do you?"

It was a question I was not prepared to be asked. "Do I what?"

"Do you want to fuck your husband?" Dr. Sinclair asks.

I tense … and then channel Eden. "I like how sex feels … orgasms. I like giving them, too, watching him."

"Physically, you enjoy sex."

I, as Eden, nod.

"Do you love … your husband?" Her voice trails off as if she is searching for his name.

"James."

"Do you love James?"

"Of course I do. I have to, so I do," I say.

"Why do you have to?"

"We're married." I hear the sadness in my voice. I hate that, but it's honest.

"What does marriage mean to you?"

"Unlimited sex … financial splits."

Dr. Sinclair's face tightens at that, like a piece of herself has been revealed … some of her *own* personal honesty.

It's the first really cold day in New York, and I am comforted by it. I look out the window and watch the leaves making their way off their branches and down onto the sidewalk, baring the trees. Much like how I feel in this office: slowly shedding layers of myself through Eden.

I gather therapy is much the same: like trees baring themselves of each leaf, each trauma, heartache, disappointment, dream, fear. I once read that autumn is a symbol of hope for trauma survivors: it proves how something beautiful can fall apart and blossom again. It's a reminder to have hope, to know that in due time, the trees will be full again, and so will we.

Dr. Sinclair remains quiet.

She is wearing a white button up top with a thick knit cardigan over it. She has a gold necklace delicately hanging from her neck that sits just above the button. I don't know why I concern myself with the button possibly ripping the charm off her necklace. It looks like a gold heart with diamonds. I can't see it clearly, but it glistens as she shifts position.

Like the first time I saw her, she is pretty plain. Not pretty. *Just* plain. Her hair is flat, and even if she ran a comb through it, it would still appear stringy and dry. She is wearing glasses different from those she had on during our first session—rectangular with a red pattern on the top and side of the rim.

The gold band around her ring finger on her left hand makes my stomach tighten. I look down at my own band and think of Miller. I replay what I just said: marriage is unlimited sex and financial splits.

In this moment, I miss Miller deeply. It feels different from missing him *desperately*, as if he's the oxygen I need to breathe. This is more profound—like he is the soul I will find again and again, in every lifetime. I miss the sex, sure, but I miss the love and friendship far more. There was a time when he was my best friend.

"You look lost in thought, Eden," Dr. Sinclair says. She emphasizes *Eden*.

I shake my head. "Just thinking. Processing and gathering information."

She nods. "So, marriage is unlimited sex and financial splits. That's where we were."

I nod.

"What was it like at the beginning of the marriage?" she asks. "For Eden and James."

I give Dr. Sinclair a brief outline, conversationally: Eden and James meet on a flight. He is off-duty and very sexy. The "*Who wouldn't want to fuck him?*" type. Outside of the bedroom, though, there is no chemistry. They don't run in the same social circles, and they have different schedules, interests, and backgrounds. Eventually, marriage seems like the only logical option, to keep up the charade.

"So, marriage is a farce?" Dr. Sinclair interrupts. "A fake? For you?"

"I guess so, yeah."

"Tell me a little about your history, Eden. Your childhood, caregivers …"

"My father left when I was a kid. My mom was an addict, married my stepdad, who was an alcoholic, and they hit each other," I begin. "But not in the way it's portrayed on TV. My father hit my mother, and she'd hit him right back. She stabbed him with a knife more than once, in his shoulder and his leg. I guess she didn't actually want to kill him. She threw the microwave at him once … another time, a large plate."

"And where were you when these things happened?"

"Sometimes in the room, but I don't think they noticed. Sometimes, in my room. I'd cry and beg for them to stop, but they just ignored me. It was like I was invisible." I use some of what I remember from the domestic violence survivors I'd heard from during my research for *The Convent* here. Eden is not too different from Jillian.

"Where did you live?"

"California. Venice Beach, Santa Cruz … always the poor sections."

"What is the earliest memory you have of your parents?"

I contemplate for a moment, because I, Diana, haven't thought of that. "Drinking and laughing. What they did looked …"

"Fun?"

I nod.

"And what would you do, while they fought?"

"Sometimes just watch TV, sometimes just cry, sometimes throw up, sometimes hide under my bed. It depends on when it started."

"What did they do with you?"

"What do you mean?"

"When you cried or threw up?"

"Nothing."

"Nothing?"

I shake my head. "That's the problem. The problem is *nothing happened.*"

Dr. Sinclair nods compassionately, closing her eyes and unfolding her hands.

"You blocked out the trauma and had to take care of yourself at an early age? So, with James, what I'm hearing is that you associate marriage with anything but love and friendship. It has conditions: drinking and laughing, chaos, unlimited sex, splitting the bills."

I nod. All out of questions, after a few minutes of silence, Dr. Sinclair says, "So, I want to go over a few basics with you about psychopaths and emotions, if you would like to."

She wants to talk to Diana. I nod.

"Psychopaths exhibit more curiosity and are less analytical about what happens to them or is happening around them."

"Did I do s-something wrong?" I accidentally stammer. I haven't since I was a child.

"No, no. Oh, I apologize. Some of what I'm hearing feels more emotionally reactive. If Eden's husband is cheating on her, she'd react a bit more with a sense of feeling out of control or being humiliated by him—she may even be in *competition* with him."

"Competition with him over what?" I ask.

She tilts her head to the side, pondering my question. "Authority, I'd say," she says.

I nod, partially understanding but partially wanting to say, *I already told you she wants revenge.* But I'm here for help, not to be a know-it-all. "Thank you," is all I say. The words taste like venom in my mouth. "I think I got it."

"Are you sure?"

"Mm-hmm."

"Okay."

The room is silent.

"Same time, same place?" she says, confirming our next session.

I nod, stand, and walk out.

CHAPTER FIVE
DIANA

Miller texts something about an afterschool meeting. He won't be home until after six, and says that I should fix something for myself if I'm hungry. I don't respond. I reach for the remote, launch Amazon, and click on *Hart to Hart,* an 80's show I have been binging. The episode title: "What Murder?"

I think back to when Miller couldn't wait to get home. When he would practically rush out of work, because "I went too long without a kiss, and my lips are lonely." I haven't heard that line in years.

Miller and I met through mutual friends. I was twenty-four, and he was twenty-seven.

My best friend, Lori, who left the city for San Diego five years ago, worked as the history teacher where Miller was assistant principle. She was badgering me to go out for drinks with her colleagues. "You need to get out there," she said. It was easy for her to say: she was newly engaged. My first relationship—one that had lasted five years—ended when my ex-boyfriend found out his high school girlfriend had moved back to their hometown and was single.

According to Lori, I should have moved on faster than I did. It's always the "taken" friends who say that. But it wasn't that simple; Ben and I had built a life together. We dated throughout college, moved in together during our senior year, and talked about getting married when we were comfortable in our careers. We wanted two dogs, one baby to give all of our love to, and talked about moving somewhere warm. But less than two weeks after Ben heard that Christina was back in Cincinnati, he was gone. I stalked him on MySpace (when it was still popular) and cried at the adorable pictures of them apple-picking, wine-tasting, and concert-going. They bought a house after just three months. I guess his *'Let's wait until our finances are good and we are both secure at work before buying a place"* line was bullshit.

While looking for a place in the city, I lived with Lori in her small two-bedroom in Stuyvesant Town on the Lower East Side. I rented out the spare bedroom for $400 a month. I had not planned on living in Manhattan or Brooklyn (the only boroughs I had any interest in at all), but the city grew on me. New York is the one and only place in the world where you can be yourself, and no one will pay you any mind. When I was not at the bodega ordering two medium coffees and looking for more freelancing work, I drank and slept. Drank. And slept.

"I'm fine staying in and having a drink here." I took a bottle of Disaronno from the top cabinet shelf.

"This," she took it out of my hand, "is mine." She smiled, implying she didn't actually mind if I drank it. "You need to come out … there are far better ones out there than that POS."

"You never said anything about Ben being a piece of shit while I was dating him."

"How he left you makes him a piece of shit—good relationship or not. I do get it, but it has been almost a year. You can miss someone and still get out there again. You are only twenty-four, and this is *New York City*. You'll find others."

"Easy for you to say," I mumbled under my breath.

"I know it's hard for you," she said. "You think of your dad and how …"

"Lori, stop!" I did not need a shrink, or to be reminded of my father, who left my mother when she told him she was pregnant, in that moment. Lori walked out of the room, and for a split moment, I felt guilty. She was only trying to help.

"I'm sorry," she said, returning.

"Me too."

She was right. Lori was almost always right.

I sucked it up, pulled my hair back into a high bun, found

my most slim-fitting pair of black jeans, a black silk top, and ankle boots with a heel, and put on some makeup. I truly did not want to waste my twenties pining over Ben … the kind of man I didn't want to be with again. But Lori was right; his abandonment had struck an old wound—the one my father left. I just didn't want to feel it.

We went to a new and eclectic bar in mid-town called Mad-Hatten. It was the type of place you'd expect to see Samantha Jones at the top of the guest list as opposed to a colleague get-together, I thought. But it wasn't my place to judge. I anxiously sipped a Moscow Mule as Lori introduced me to her coworkers, Jackie and Lizette. Soon after, six more people trickled in back-to-back. Miller was one of them—*the best looking one.*

"I'm a writer." These were the words that left my lips with each introduction.

Most of them praised me for being brave enough to pursue a creative field … for going after my dreams. Miller was the only one who asked what kind of writing I did.

"Everything," I told him.

"Oh, I was worried you were going to be vague, but 'everything'!"

I frowned a little, embarrassed.

"I didn't mean for that to be rude." He frowned, too, like he had recognized the awkwardness of his tone. "Tell me more about this 'everything.'"

I took a sip of my almost-empty mojito. "No, sorry. It's okay. I wasn't offended or anything. I do a bit of freelance—different fiction and non-fiction pieces for various publicat-ions. Trying to find my place, I guess. I mean, I *can* write anything, *everything*—well, maybe except for Sci-Fi or Fant-asy—I am not very good at creating a world from scratch. Like cities, countries, politics, things like that, but I enjoy writing almost everything. I want to write novels." My morti-fication increased as I rambled on. "Sorry. This probably sounds like an interview."

Miller shook his head. "No, I think that's really cool. I'd love to read something you've written. Show me."

"What?"

"Pull something up."

In that moment, I noticed how we had completely aband-oned the group. Miller and I were at one end of the bar while Lori and the rest were enmeshed in a conversation at the other. It had been a while since I had dated, and I was afraid I had conducted myself like some sort of idiot in front of him. He was also way too gorgeous to be single, so I was worried he was humoring me. The truth is, I wanted to date again, but I didn't feel good enough. Plain and simple.

"You don't have to read anything. It's okay," I said.

He looked offended and took a sip of his drink.

"I mean, really? You wanna read something?" I asked, skeptically.

He nodded and brushed his fingers along the top of my hand that was trembling on the counter. With that same hand, I pulled out my Blackberry and pulled up an email I had sent to my editor containing the final draft of my latest piece. Miller read it intently, not drawing away from it even to take a sip of his drink. "You're … this is really good."

"Really? You think?"

He raised an eyebrow. "You got me with the first sentence: *I'm too fragile and delicate to be loved.* I think we all feel that way. I got to the end and was disappointed there wasn't more."

I smile. *Writers love to hear that.*

"Why were you sitting over here away from the group?" he asked.

"Large crowds make me anxious these days," I said. "Lori was hell-bent on getting me out of the house, though."

"Why's that?"

I wasn't sure how to answer, so I shrugged. "She thinks I need to get out there."

He sighed. "I hate that phrase. It makes me *not* want to get out there."

"Exactly!" I noticed how excited I got, so I switched my demeanor, along with the subject. "How do you like being a principal?"

"Assistant," he clarified. "Hopefully, I'll get there one day. I love working in education. I've always wanted to help people." He placed air quotes around the word *help* and rolled his eyes, indicating embarrassment. "So I figured why not help them at an early age, through their education?" He paused for a moment before adding, "Do you want children?"

I was caught off guard, and I think he noticed, because he quickly apologized.

"No, it's fine. I'd love one, to be honest."

He nodded. "Me too."

I smiled. I had only considered having one child with Ben, because that's what he wanted. The truth was, after learning how my father had asked my mother for an abortion and subsequently feeling like my mother was *forced* to love me, I wasn't sure I wanted kids at all. I was happy to give Ben one, but when Miller said he couldn't wait to have his own, I suddenly felt myself wanting to give him a dozen, despite the fact we had only just met.

"At the risk of being too forward, any chance I could give you a call? Maybe take you out this weekend?" he asked.

I internally smiled. *He was single.*

Miller and I dated for three years before we got married. He healed something in me he didn't break. Something I didn't know needed healing. I never had a home before him. I secured a job as a columnist and began the outline for my first book during those years, and Miller was promoted to principal of a middle school downtown. We traveled to countries in Europe and Asia during July, when he was off for a few weeks, and made the mistake of visiting the United Arabs Emirates during one of their hottest months. Still, we made the most out of such a once-in-a-life-time vacation. It was a beautiful and fulfilling way to see the world together at such a young age. Though my desire to give him a dozen kids never left my mind, we didn't feel the need to rush into parenthood. So, we waited a few years before trying for a baby.

In the meantime, I hoped to publish a book or two, and Miller had his own goals to achieve. We truly enjoyed life, just the two of us.

One day in Athens, he caught me buying an adorable onesie. He thought bringing something back from each of our trips for our future babies was a sweet idea.

We decided to try for a baby around the time I was writing *The Convent.* I'd hoped to complete it beforehand, but I figured nine months would give me enough time to research and write.

Getting pregnant was easy; preserving a pregnancy was difficult. Miscarriage after miscarriage consumed me with worry about having waited too long. Time was something we felt was on our side—we were invincible, in that respect. That is, until four years passed, complete with six failed pregnancies. I felt naïve, thinking it would happen on the first try.

Life quickly became consumed by doctor visits, ovulation mapping, scheduled sex, and the inevitable bloodstain.

"I have to lie on my back with my legs up," I told him. I usually liked being on top. I got off him and rolled over, assuming the position. "Okay, go."

"Okay, go?" he repeated.

I rolled my eyes. "Come on, don't be like that. I have to be relaxed for this to work." He was standing on the floor; I was on the edge of the bed. Miller knelt down between my legs and put his mouth on me. "Uh-uh," I nudged him away, despite the pleasure.

"You said you needed to be relaxed."

"I need to get pregnant! Come on, just do it." He looked hurt, disappointed, but I didn't care. "Don't you want this, too?"

"I don't know anymore."

"You have to!"

"I have," he said. "I've also done my part!"

Immediately, I broke down in tears. I knew what he was saying: it was me, my body, my inability to carry to term. He had done his part; I couldn't do mine. I felt humiliated, broken.

"Di, I'm sorry. Oh, my love, I'm so, so sorry. Please don't

cry," he said. He leaned over the bed, lowering my dress, and kissed me. "We'll do this. I didn't mean to make you cry."

"Why can't I do this? Why am I broken?"

He put his hand on my belly. "You're not broken, Di. It'll happen. We can do it in whatever position you want. You can hang upside down, if you want. We'll get some sort of jungle gym thing to … hey, wait." He paused to smirk. "That sounds kinda hot." I laughed through my tears. "What can I do?" he asked softly.

"Promise that if this never happens for us, you will still love me." I wiped my wet face with my arms before pulling him close to my chest. "Please don't ever leave me because of this. I love you so much."

"I promise. I love you today just as much as I did the day we got married."

We started kissing, and he laid on his back. "You like it on top. Come on. I promise I'll flip you over before I finish."

A month later, I got my period.

We tried again.

I got pregnant. Then, four months later, I miscarried.

The same routine.

Miller opted against adoption, and I opted against surrogacy. After two years, we took a break from trying. It's mentally easier to get your period when you expect it.

I wrote and finished *Mathilde*, and around the same time, I learned I was pregnant again. This time, I carried the baby to term. But our daughter was stillborn.

Everything changed; I became angry and empty. *We* became angry and empty. Miller couldn't control his temper, and I shut down. *Our new routine.* I slept through most days … didn't even attend my own book release party. Miller and I kept out of each other's way. My room was filled with empty bottles and plates still full of food until Miller was eventually forced to clean them up. I only got out of bed to use the toilet and take the occasional shower. Most nights, he slept in the guest room.

"Go," I said one day when he tried to coax me out of bed. "Go find another woman who can give you everything you want … someone who isn't so depressed. Please. Just go. Go have your life." I didn't mean it, but I didn't want him to be as unhappy as I was, either.

"*You* are the life I want," he consoled me. "I told you before: I love you today just as much as I did the day we got married." He held me as we both cried. Our tears spoke the words we couldn't.

Not many months later, I built up the strength to venture back out into the world. Three years of depression wore out our apartment, so we hired a housekeeper, and I saw a psychiatrist. I needed uppers and downers to get up, and to drown out my thoughts and memories. I was ninety-six pounds at thirty-nine years old. I'd eat, feel guilty for gaining weight, and purge it out of me. I didn't want my stomach to grow in any way. I missed the comfort of life moving inside of me. Eventually, I saw an eating specialist. I got healthier, but still couldn't escape myself.

That was three years ago.

I know Miller resents me, because *I* resent me. I think he stays with me out of pity. And as degrading as it sounds, I am okay with that. I am still so in love with him. I wish it could be enough.

We have lost all forms of intimacy: the connection, laughs, jokes, and overall life in our relationship. *Key components*. It feels like we're roommates who share a bed. Yet there is no one else I would rather share a bed with … no one else I would rather struggle through this with, than Miller. I hope he feels the same. On the flip side, I have seen how child loss plays out in a marriage: the couple rarely stays together. So, maybe he doesn't stay with me out of pity. Maybe he does not resent me, but accepts me. And that means everything.

It is probably selfish of me to not ask for a divorce when I think he might be unhappy. He likely wants out, or feels stuck, and I know it. But isn't it also selfish for him to want out?

I have lost everything about myself. I've lost the family I had hoped to birth.

I cannot lose Miller.

I will not.

Lying on the couch with Lucy and Ethel snuggled beside me, I try to push the thoughts of babies and Miller out of my mind, but I have been doing so for so long, it feels like a balloon held under water: if you release the pressure, the only way it can go is back up to the surface.

I used to dread days like this, being with my own thoughts, but that does not happen much anymore. I don't know if I am used to the pain, or if what they say is true—that time heals wounds. I have never really believed that, though. It's the work you do that heals. *Or perhaps it's the avoidance.*

I re-read the text from Miller, about the curriculum meeting running late, and to not wait for him for dinner.

I close it, sigh, and refocus my attention back on *Hart to Hart* just in time to hear one of the character's say, "The day is still young, and I'm sure, so is she."

CHAPTER SIX
MAUREEN

I was a bit anxious when a woman called my office with quite the unusual request—to be profiled as someone else. I have never received such a proposal.

In many circumstances, I get excited when the word *psychopath* or *psychopathy* comes up. I left the field of neuropsychology to become a therapist, an area in which I thought I could do more productive and hands-on work to help others enrich their lives. But I do miss the days I spent studying and working in psychopathy. After all, a psychopath cannot be "cured."

Forgive me for using that word.

We doctors generally stay far away from it. The goal is to help heal, repair, and aid. But a psychopath is different from most clients. For one, a *true* psychopath would never *be* a client. He or she would seldom willingly undergo therapy. Just like how neither you nor I could grow a set of wings (though how lovely a thought), a psychopath cannot grow a conscience. Emotions. *How utterly fascinating.* That concept both drew me to the specialty and pushed me out of it.

Rather than hiring me for services or because she wanted me to do a presentation, she proposed something else entirely. "I'm writing a book," she explained, "about a female serial killer. She targets her husbands, for various but—in her mind—justifiable reasons. It begins with a plot to kill her new husband, and I'm still working out the details, but I would like to get into the psychology of a serial killer, of psychopaths, since I'll be writing her as one. I would like to be profiled as my character."

I made a few affirming noises as she spoke, so she knew I was following and listening. "Sounds compelling," I told her. Though truthfully, her request, not the plot, sounded a bit rubbish to me. Still, I found myself asking, "Can you elaborate more on the profiling part?"

"I'm preparing my research material and need a lot of clinical feedback. Because I'm still in the developmental stage, I'd like to come in and talk as if I am her."

I tilt my head, confused. "Talk as her? To gain my expertise?"

"That, yes, and ..." She paused, for emphasis or due to nerves, I didn't know. "I'd like you to *treat me* as if I really am Eden Lowell, my protagonist."

Despite Diana accepting to pay my fee of two hundred and fifty per session, I was unsure how to respond to her request. I have been approached for my expertise in the past, especially since I have done a lot of research on criminals and psychopaths, but this went far beyond those types of requests.

"I'm a bit anxious, but curious and intrigued, as well," I said. "I think I have an idea about how I can help, but why don't we set up an appointment to meet in person and talk about the profiling part a little bit more?" As a freelancer, Diana said, she was blessed with time and would be there. Her tone was confident and excited. I wondered her age. Perhaps early thirties.

***

During our initial consultation, I learned that Diana Steinbeck is a New York native and graduate of Syracuse University, with a bachelor's in journalism and master's in English. I was surprised to hear she is forty-three years old. She does not look her age, with her slim figure, shiny, healthy-looking blonde hair that brushes her shoulders and glowing skin. Except, perhaps, for her eyes. They were covered by thin-rimmed, black glasses. I note the dark circles under them. My guess: a deep sadness.

Surprised she is older than me, albeit by three years, I felt self-conscious about the wrinkles creasing my eyes and gray strands of hair exposed amongst the red. She is aging gracefully, whereas I look like my mum—and my mum has been dead for twenty years.

"I'm not sure if you heard of me before." Diana paused. Her face softened, but her eyes remained focused on me as if expecting me to say, *Yes, of course. You're the famous Diana ... Ross or Princess Diana.* But to me, she was just Diana: the writer who needs consulting. Before I had the chance to respond, she continued. "I've written a few bestsellers." Diana shifted her position in the chair, patted down her brown trousers and tucked one hand under her thigh. A sign of nervousness. She sat at the chair at my desk, preferring not to sit on the couch until she's Eden. "*The Convent* is my most popular book."

"Unfortunately, I don't have much time for reading," I said. Which was the truth. I don't. Not with a full-time job and two little girls. My reading consists of *How to Catch a Unicorn, The Giving Tree*, and *Amelia Bedelia* ... or the latest article on psychopathy, when I can fit one in. In bed, I'm lucky if I'm able to skim my husband's body, let alone a book. Of course, I didn't say any of this to Diana.

She nodded, expressionless, removed her hand from under her thigh, and lifted both up like she was waiting to be handed something large and delicate. "I know it's unorthodox, but I think if I immerse myself into my character, really become her, I will write more poetically and practically."

I was charmed by her use of language. "I have never been approached with such an offer," I said. "I'm willing to try it with grace and flexibility. While it is a business exchange, not a traditional therapeutic setting, I would feel more comfortable if the same ethical rules apply here as they would in a *traditional* setting. If I'm uncomfortable with how it's going or find I can't be of help, I can refer you to a colleague perhaps better suited for this particular situation."

"I understand and appreciate your clarity and honesty." Another expressionless nod.

"Shall we schedule your first session?"

Diana nodded.

Curious, I asked if she met with any other psychologists or specialists.

"I have. Two. Like I said, if I am to present Eden as a psychopath, it is a rare diagnosis, and I know you did extensive work in that field."

I nodded. "It *is* a rare diagnosis because we usually don't, forgive me, but we usually don't find them until they have committed a crime. Not all psychopaths are violent, though. Some people in my field believe they shouldn't be called or labeled 'psychopaths' at all, as it's technically not part of the

DSM—the Diagnostic and Statistical Manual of Mental Disorders—in which we are meant to characterize them based on other criteria and personality traits. The *correct* term is antisocial personality disorder."

I didn't know why I was rambling on as I dug for my small red organizer I keep in the drawer of the table next to my chair.

"What makes the diagnosis rare?" Diana asked quietly, like a little girl.

"There are many false narratives out there," I said, and continued on to explain the statistics. She nodded a thank you, and I flipped open the pages to look at my coming weeks before going to my monthly calendar. Almost at full capacity, and not really taking on new clients, I asked Diana for a minute while I sorted through my schedule. "Do Thursdays at one work?"

She took her phone out of her small black purse, the light illuminated her face, scrolled for a minute and said. "Yes. See you next Thursday."

***

My first sessions with Diana, the questions and roleplaying, were strange for me—but at the same time, I felt some addictive quality about them. The newness of it both intrigues and worries me.

Following my session with her today—learning about Eden's marriage and childhood—I had three back to back clients.

At the end of my day, I sigh deeply. I am mentally drained—rather, mentally *full*. We are all prone to burnout, but it is critical for my clients that I manage my time and schedule in a way that allows me to give them my full attention. Tonight, however, I feel different.

I decide to walk home, nearly forty blocks, but I do it so often, I have become immune to the distance. I put my AirPods in and blast some instrumental music; I do not want to hear any voices, so it helps me drown out as much as possible for the duration of the walk. By the time I reach home, I am exhausted. I have not felt much like myself over the last day or two—stomachache and fatigue—and all I want to do is lay down. It is the impossible dream all mums of young children entertain stepping into their flat: that they will get some peace and quiet.

When tummies are full and the bath water starts to cool, I try to get my girls into bed early. Another impossible dream. My husband, Adam, keeps to himself in our dual office, which had been a spare bedroom prior to the pandemic. I know he isn't working right now … more likely, he is finishing off the Jack Daniels he stores in the cabinet above the refrigerator. He thinks I don't know about it … just as I don't think he knows about my own stash in the hallway closet, behind the winter shoes.

We don't have a drinking problem, just problems. And we are responsible, especially when our daughters are around. I can count the number of times they have seen us drink on one hand. Though lately, it's been harder and harder to avoid. I admit, I've snuck into the closet and office one too many times myself over the last couple of months.

Guilt, or a *celebration of my secrets*? The same secrets that nearly cost me my marriage, my children, and my own sanity. The ones that contributed to a former client's institutionalization. And when I think of *those* memories, it is three glasses a night. I wonder if that's what Adam is doing right now—savoring his secrets in each sip of bourbon as it runs down his throat, spicy and sweet. I wonder what kind of secrets he carries with him, the ones he sheds off before climbing into bed with me.

I push those thoughts out of my head as I tend to my youngest daughter, Eloise, who cannot fall asleep. And thus, my eldest, Jane, can't either. I call Adam in to help me; I need to lie down.

"What story do you want me to read?" he asks Eloise, walking in.

"No stories, Adam." I roll off the bed. Eloise sits up to

chime in. "We are trying to get her to *sleep*. It's almost eleven." He doesn't listen, plucking three books from the shelf. He asks Eloise to choose one, and she picks all three.

"Adam, what did I just say?"

"Bedtime stories help kids fall asleep," he says. He leans in to Eloise, looks up at me, makes eye contact, and whispers, "Mum's a bit of a crank tonight, isn't she?"

I hate when he calls me "*Mum.*" He is not English, which makes it feel like he is mocking me, though I know he isn't. I also hate that he calls me a "crank" in front of our daughters. He has gotten into the habit of making these kinds of slightly rude comments in front of our girls, perhaps knowing I won't react strongly in front of them.

Eloise giggles.

Jane looks uncomfortable as she tosses and turns in her twin bed, with a floral-patterned comforter, on the opposite side of the room. I walk over to her, and she pauses, lies flat on her back. I ask her if she wants a glass of water. She doesn't. I apologize for her father keeping her up and give her a kiss on the head. I brush her silky, strawberry-blonde hair back from her face, a small curl bounces, and her brown eyes reflecting against the star-shaped nightlight. "Do you want me to rub your back?"

She smiles, as though she is trying to comfort me, and says, "I'm fine." She has a slight English accent and takes after me. Eloise doesn't. She takes after her father, I guess.

I wait nearly an hour for Adam to come to bed. I don't know why, since I can hardly keep my eyes open, but when he does, he leans over to kiss me, and I shift my body away. "It isn't fair to Jane. You keep her up." I enunciate each word.

Adam tosses his clothes on the cushioned bench in front of our bed and plops down on the mattress, causing it to shake. "You want Eloise up all night and in our bed? I know how much you hate that," he replies. He says it spitefully, as if it's wrong to want space while I sleep.

Eloise's first "big girl" bed was really ours. She would climb out of her crib and crawl in with us, which was the *only* way she would sleep. This went on for two years. If we tried to keep her in her room, she would throw tantrums and fake cough until she'd vomit. The fight was not worth her physical or mental health. Considering my line of work, I felt guilty about being unable to help her. I did not want her medicated, so I listened to her and succumbed to her sleeping with us. So, every night, our two-year-old climbed into our bed until she finally (somewhat) grew out of it.

It was hard for Adam and me to be intimate. We found ways; had sex in the shower sometimes, but it wasn't very comfortable or practical. At night, I was worried Eloise would walk in on us, so we just started putting her in bed with us at the start of the night. I missed sleeping alone with my husband—emphasis on sleeping—and our sex life. Adam understood, but considered Eloise's wants before our own needs, which made me feel undesired as a wife and like an inconsiderate mother. Of course, *he* was getting enough sleep. He wasn't the one Eloise kept up with her pleas for "one more" song or story.

The irony didn't escape me, either, considering his line of work—Adam is a relationship therapist at the Manhattan Couples Center. My friends have asked me, "Isn't it weird to have your husband talking about sex with other women? Such intimate details?" In response, I would joke that as long as he was having sex with me, and only me, it did not bother me. But I admit that during the first couple of months of dating, I had similar questions in my head, and it was hard to ignore. If I was not in the business, I would have been more skeptical.

I don't know the particulars around what he talks about with his patients, nor do I care to. It's the nature of our work. Any good mental health professional refrains from talking about patients with family or friends. That's not to say that I haven't witnessed some of my own therapist friends sit in a bar and disclose easily identifiable case details. But to me, it's a big turn-off. Our patients trust us, and we are morally obligated to uphold that level of trust, with or without them knowing.

Adam, however, is very perceptive, which makes him a

great confidant. Especially when I have a particularly difficult day or reoccurring issue. For example, one of my younger patients constantly lied to me. Over several sessions, she went on and on about a traumatic event, just to later admit she had made the whole thing up. She then retracted her admission, begging me to believe her. There was a deeper meaning to the lying, but no matter how I tried to unpack it, I remained stuck. So, I asked Adam for his professional opinion. I found his advice insightful and helpful.

This doesn't happen often, though. Ethics aside, neither of us really want to discuss our patients. Which is a relief, honestly. I feared we would have nothing to talk about. Fortunately, we enjoy talking about our girls, traveling, moving, current events, politics … *our own issues* … a lot more. And that's refreshing, after six or seven clients per day. It's better to be in your own mind.

And out of it.

There are times, though, when it is difficult to leave work at work, as anyone in pretty much any field can attest. When I was pregnant with Eloise six years ago, I saw a patient whose son was diagnosed with leukemia. She was not like the clients I normally take on, but she had been referred to me. I was the sixth clinician she had met with, and I knew how I could help her. Sometimes, after a session or two, I would look down at my belly and hope my baby would never be diagnosed with a terminal illness and pass away, like Tommy eventually did.

The first thing they tell you when you study psychology is not to self-diagnose. You can get caught up in the symptoms, criteria, and diagnoses, and all of the sudden, you are a depressed, malignant, borderline narcissist sociopath. Of course, I am none of these. Just depressed and a little anxious. This can also happen with the patients we see. Patients trigger a lot of memories and emotions and things we run from, too, and it is critical to avoid creating an enmeshment of emotions and issues. In severe cases, when a therapist is unable to do so, this causes the therapist to subconsciously project her personal issues onto the client and work through them. A very dangerous place to be, which is why self-awareness is the most vital aspect of being a psychotherapist.

Trust me when I say you want a therapist who is self-aware.

And with a life of her own.

At Cambridge, I studied education and psychology before I moved to New York City, where I got my Ph.D from New York University. Psychology was not a field I just fell into. I had a longing to study human behavior and how I could help others, particularly children, since I was not much more than a child myself. But after seeing some horrific things—like an eleven-year-old's suicide attempt that left her neck so badly bruised from the wet towel she used as a noose, I feared her purple and red veins would pop, and an eight-year-old boy's attempt at drowning Ryder, the family dog in the bathtub without a bit of remorse—I shifted my focus to adults.

I was not turned off by these children. The opposite, in fact. I wanted to take them all home with me and give them the love they felt (and were) so deprived of. I could not sit with Ella and her bruised neck and not feel compelled to do more than what was happening in our therapy room. I admired my colleagues who could.

During my education, I became increasingly fascinated with the human brain, so I concentrated on neuropsychology: the study of brain functionality—the relationship between the brain and behavior. I worked in hospitals under neuropsychologists and neuroscientists studying psychopathy. Though psychopaths make up a very small portion of our society, at one point, it seemed they were all around me.

My interest was rooted in their lack of remorse and empathy—how hollow they are. It is an interesting concept, *to be empty*. There is feeling numb, and then there is a total lack of emotion, which is something else entirely. I had once used pills and alcohol as a means to numbness, but I took back my *I wish I didn't feel* when I was faced with individuals who did not have a choice. I was saddened for them, especially knowing they would never know how deeply my colleagues and I felt for them. It was the acceptance of those intense emotions that led me back to my original goal of being a psycho-therapist with my own practice.

Adam and I met at scheduled consults between several practicing therapists about ten years ago.

He is much taller than me, a little over six foot, and I found that attractive. His big hands and long fingers that cradled his Starbucks coffee during our Friday morning meetings, along with his sharp features and prominent cheek bones, made a lasting impression on me. It was, and still is, easy to read his emotions by the way he clenches his jaw.

During our meetings, he talked passionately. Whether about his own patients or the slightest concern about a patient, he never held back. I found that attractive, too, and made the first move.

"You seem really upset today," I said as we left the building. The elevator was crowded, so we took the two flights of stairs down. "Would you like to get something to eat and talk some more?" I didn't really want to talk about the patient whose case was so upsetting him, but I *really* liked him … it felt like an all-encompassing schoolgirl crush. I wasn't even sure what else to say to get the chance to spend more time with him.

"The guy said he loved his mother, sister, his–" he paused, glancing around cautiously before whispering, "fucking *car* more than his wife. In front of her. I wanted to slug him."

I laughed. *I would've too*, I wanted to say.

"I wanted to tell her to run for the hills," he went on.

"Yeah, I hear you. Objectiveness is difficult. It's also not easy to find the good in everyone, but it's possible." That was all I managed to say, and I felt like an imbecile.

He took a sip of water. "Actually, it isn't really difficult, for me. I just remind myself that the hardest patients to work with are the ones who need empathy and love the most. Even this guy."

I rested my chin in my hand and smiled.

Love.

I was falling.

"You really are a dick," I say to him now. "You know that, right?" I sit up in bed, still feeling sick. "You would rather have Jane, who *won't* come in our bed because she doesn't want to bother us, up all night?"

Adam rolls his eyes. "Yeah. *Us*."

"What are you going on about?"

He puts his phone in the charging dock, and I hear the "ding" notification. He has a habit of checking the *Post* before he goes to sleep and just as he wakes up. "Jane doesn't want to bother *you,* Ree. She's trying to be perfect for you."

"That's absurd." I feel the warmth of my cheeks as they

flush. "Eloise worships the ground *you* walk on because you give her everything."

I am aware that I'm engaged in a little "Who-Is-Screwing-Up-Our-Kids-More" battle, but I can't help it. One day, Adam and I were partners—a team, a pair—and the next, it was all about how I had fallen short of my duties as a mother and my expectation as a wife—as if it's 1952.

"I give her a father."

Do I not give her a mother? Is that what he thinks? I want to ask, but I am afraid I already know the answer. I think of my own father, who passed away when I was five. Mum would not tell me what from. She and I moved from Brighton to Manchester, where she later passed away from breast cancer just before I went off to university. We had been very close, but I felt a hostility toward her for rarely having talked about my father. I sometimes still hold resentment. My dimmest memories of him are in our backyard. He loved picking flowers and holding them to my cheek, which he did when he would apologize to me, though I cannot remember what for.

Mum was much happier alone than when she was with my father. She worked at the local bookstore and knew everyone in our neighborhood. She brought cakes and puddings to our elderly neighbors and gifted books to the children. She had a good, kind heart, and shortly after her passing, I had quite the breakdown. I wish I had done more for her rather than harboring resentment.

I push her and Dad out of my head as tears fill my eyes, careful not to let Adam see. I remind him I am not a patient and do not need him to school me on my own daughter.

He corrects me: *our* daughter.

"Whatever," I say. I finish applying my eye cream and slither further under the comforter, roll onto my right side, and shut off the light.

A few moments later, Adam slides over to me, pressing his body onto mine as he kisses my cheek. "I'm sorry. But they're only so little for so long."

I move away from him.

"Is something going on?" he asks. "Are you having another one of your–"

Episodes, he was going to say. He thinks by accepting my "episodes," aka breakdowns, and forgiving me for my infidelities, he can use them against me, or to one up me. In reality, we both know it's a way of manipulating the situation to ensure he is in full control … a *leave before I'm left* approach.

What is going on is, I am not attracted to him anymore.

What is going on is, I want to leave him.

What is going on is, I can't leave him.

What is going on is, I am trying not to fall madly in love with another man.

What is going on is, *I am* falling madly in love with

another man.

The fear of being alone can change someone, make them behave like someone other than themselves. Sometimes, we can't escape it, we are wired to be together, as humans. Loneliness is as real as the toxic relationships we hang onto. Therefore, I sometimes think Adam and I are following the norm. The status quo. Career, marriage, babies. In that order.

But is that what we really want? What I really want? I love and want my girls, of course, but … is this all there is to the rest of my life?

I want to scream. A part of me thinks I should … that it might actually be the best thing for us. Instead, I respond calmly, flatly. "I'm not having another anything."

He doesn't respond. I want to explain more about how I'm feeling, but I'm too overcome with sickness, like I might vomit. I need to sleep. So, I close my eyes and do just that.

CHAPTER SEVEN
MAUREEN

After discussing the fact that most psychopaths are high functioning and *not* murderous villains—a bias society has on the word psychopath—and some of the cranial science behind psychopathy with Diana, a strange sense of familiarity settled over me.

The concept of psychopathy returned to me in a form I didn't expect: a memory of my first boyfriend, Joseph. I moved in with him within six months of meeting him. I needed a place to stay, and he needed a girl to take his anger out on. He smacked me around, but never hard enough to leave a mark.

One night, I brought home an abandoned kitty I found on the side of the road. Two days later, Cottie's throat was slit. Joseph said she had been "purring too much." I cried for days. I assumed he really did it because I had arrived home hours late from visiting a friend in Reading, a town about an hour away. I was to blame.

During our second semester, a string of new, young girls came to uni. They were very popular amongst the boys, and shortly after, rumors about sex parties circulated.

One evening, Joseph made a slip-of-the-tongue confession to killing one of them—suffocating her while she was drinking, causing her to choke on her own vomit—because she made fun of his nerdy outward appearance. He wore big, round glasses, had an overbite that looked more like a buck tooth, and multiple blemishes on his face. I knew what he was capable of, and it frightened me. So, when the officers came to question me, I reiterated his story about Layla choking on her own vomit after drinking too much.

Through my studies, I recognized his fitting the criteria for a psychopath.

Joseph and I eventually broke up. I didn't beg or protest, even cry, when I found out he was cheating on me. I was forced to take out loans for housing at uni. Both a small and large price to pay to get him out of my life. I was traumatized by what he did to Layla, and I worried about how easily he let me off the hook. I never told anyone about him after I left uni, not even Adam. *Are you really married to someone if you don't harbor some secrets?*

I didn't focus my studies on psychopaths solely because of Joseph, but my experience did pique my curiosity.

And with Diana's research request, she reminded me of that.

I am lost in my trail of memories when my ringer goes off, indicating my last client of the day, Jeremy, has arrived. I am grateful to be taken out of my mind, away from my memories.

Jeremy has been a client of mine for the past year, and I see him twice a week. His ex-wife threatened that if he didn't go to therapy, she wouldn't allow him to see their children. He found the entire field of psychology—including everything under its umbrella—"fake," and he made a point of telling me so over and over. That is, until he finally came to realize that he had more to unpack than he originally thought.

"I just accepted I am a sociopath and moved on with my life," he explained, one month into our sessions. "No one *ever* talked about their feelings in my house ... are you kidding?" Referring to his mother's suicide when he was fourteen, he said, "It obviously hurt, but sitting around talking about my feelings wasn't going to bring her back. So why bother?" Jeremy also shared that his mother had brought him to see a psychiatrist for behavioral problems, but she was told he was "a troublemaker," and that was that. It was the seventies, sure, but I understood his aversion and distrust for psychotherapy. He was put on medication that made him physically sick, so he stuffed the pills underneath his mattress instead of taking them. Seven years later, following his mother's death, he removed them. It was around this time that his father began abusing him—usually after drinking too much.

Today, he shares he went on a date just three nights ago. *Finally*, he emphasizes. He sounds relieved, but it feels obligatory. Like he did it for someone other than himself. *For me? Did he do it to impress me?* I smile, to let him know I'm excited to hear more. "Tell me about it."

"I mean, I was obviously there, but I can't remember anything."

His memory is concerning. Something we have been working on, indicating a greater wound we have yet to uncover. "What can't you remember about it?" I ask.

"The–" he stops and looks up to the corner of the ceiling. He is locked there, like he's lost in a memory he cannot see.

"Remember what we talked about?" I ask him. "Please focus your eyes on me." His distraction sometimes delays his memory. He will bring up a new book I have added to my shelf or some inaudible argument he can hear outside of the window.

Jeremy's dark, empty eyes lock with mine, and it's like he sees right through me. I'm nervous for a second. I investigate my nerves. It isn't fear, like a deer in headlights, but absence. What *I'm* feeling isn't absence or nerves, so I know it's Jeremy's.

"Did you feel like a passenger in your own body?" I ask.

He nods.

"Can you remember how you felt about being there?"

He shakes his head. "It was a good restaurant—Italian," he stammers. "Some celebrity chef from the Food Network. It's new. Uptown, kind of near Lincoln Center."

"I'm looking for specific emotions … and you're giving me a story," I say softly. He often does this.

He nods again and sits quietly.

I start with external before the internal. "Can you remember a sound or smell?"

"Sweet."

"Sweet?"

"Doesn't make sense, though, right? Smelling pastries at an Italian restaurant."

"What do you associate pastries with?" I probe.

"Like a memory?"

"Anything. A feeling, a person … sure, a memory."

"My mother." He pauses. I wait with him in silence. I want him to lead the conversation. "She used to make madeleines. Very, *very* light ones." He uses his hands to signify how light. "Seems fitting, given her name, and she was very sweet. But my father never ate them. It broke her heart, I think."

"Why do you think that?"

He shrugs. "I don't know. Wouldn't your heart be broken if your husband didn't eat your desserts?"

"I reckon I'd want to know *why* he wouldn't. Did she ever ask him?"

He shook his head.

"How about you? How would you feel about it?"

"Anxious."

"Can you give me a little more? There's a lot of emotions under 'anxious.' Scared? Sad? Helpless? Embarrassed?"

"Rejected." He leans back, and his lips part. He's surprised himself, and his eyes lighten. He looks pleased, even. I lean back in my chair and smile. *Progress.*

"What about it felt like rejection?" I ask.

"No one ate my mother's madeleines, not even her, so I ate them all. In one sitting. 'Til I puked."

"How old were you? Six? Seven?"

"Around there. Maybe younger."

"You felt your mother's rejection from your father, so you ate the sweets?"

He nods.

"It sounds like you did a lot of feeling for your mum."

He shrugs. "I don't know. I don't want to think about it."

"Anything else?"

He doesn't say anything.

"Did you feel unacknowledged?"

He still doesn't say anything. I nod. I won't push him just yet. I return to the date. "I think," I lean forward in my chair, "that it's easy for you to reject your emotions. Your father rejected them, both with your mother and you, when he started abusing you. So, you reject yourself—your emotions, your history, yourself—and when you reject yourself, you become somewhat of a new person, but who you *really* are continues to fight to get out. So, you feel, think, smell what he does."

"Is that why I smelled sweets?"

"I think you associated your feeling of rejection with that smell. You see?"

"What am I rejecting? The woman?"

I shake my head no. "The six, seven, maybe even a little younger you."

"From what?"

I shrug to indicate I don't want to answer for him, but I am willing to provide some ideas, insights. "We'll figure it out. But life, maybe. The way your mother ended hers. The way your father did, by not living his. Maybe your ex-wife, for not being who she wanted you to be."

Jeremy's body relaxes. He takes a deep breath and closes his eyes as he exhales. He stretches his legs out and puts his hands on his knees. He'd been sitting tightly, picking at his forearm. Now, he nods and says, "I guess that makes sense."

"Does it? I want to check in with you."

"Yeah. I don't know … maybe I wanted to reject the date before she rejected me. I don't know if that makes sense."

I agree. “It makes perfect sense. How did you feel when the date ended?”

“Well, I didn’t get laid like I thought I might.” He sighs in frustration before laughing it off, like he’s embarrassed.

When Jeremy leaves, I reach for a bag of crisps I have in my desk drawer and think about Diana: did I want to continue with her, or not? I can’t decide. I don’t feel all that comfortable with a client coming in and lying to me, omitting details about herself for a character play work. Her *role playing* a psychopath. A lot can go wrong.

I text my nanny and ask if she can stay with the girls for another hour. I want to keep detailed notes about this. I also want to run my thoughts by my consult group.

CHAPTER EIGHT
MAUREEN

Six of us sit around a long, dark table sipping wine. There are always two bottles, and we each have half a glass. A cheese board sits in front of us.

We are in a huge, tall glass building right off of Bryant Park in Midtown. I have walked past the New York Public Library many times before, but this is the first time I ever *really* look at it, I am sorry to say. I admire its detailed, carved architecture.

Miranda West, an old classmate from NYU, and I remain close colleagues and friends. Two years older than me and with more experience, she also runs her own practice. Like me, she always wanted to go into the field of psychology. She works part-time in both her practice and for a clinic, and occasionally works with juvenile inmates. Almost every psychologist I know says, "I plan to work into my seventies and eighties," because of how fulfilling the work is and how the field continues to expand. But I know Miranda will. Her work ethic has inspired me to reevaluate my skills and work on several occasions.

It's in her office building off Bryant Park that our group meets in; she acquires the space for us. These meetings are like check-ins—we seek clinical feedback and support for ourselves. Doing so ensures our clients' well-being, but also any troubling cases from triggering our own personal issues.

After simple exchanges around who's been up to what, summer vacations, and kids, I start the deeper conversation. "So, I have a new client I'm not sure how to approach. I'll call her 'June.'"

"And what is June in need of?"

"She's a researcher looking for my expertise. She wants to assume the identity of a fictitious character she's writing. Essentially, to play-act."

Laurie swirls her glass in her hand and nods in fascination. "Interesting," she says.

"That was my initial feeling, too."

"And how are you feeling now?"

"A bit anxious … like I'm being set up to fail," I admit.

"In what way?" Miranda asks.

"Well, doesn't it sound like the exact opposite of what we do?"

"What do you think we do?" Miranda asks.

I don't really answer the question. Not because I don't want to, but because I really want to vent my thoughts. "If a patient lies to us about her life or parts of what happened to her … there's a reason," I say. I pause and take a sip of wine, twirling the glass in my hand for a second before continuing. "I just find it difficult to know how to talk to her, treat her, this character, if she is being someone else."

"It would be the same as meeting someone new, only she's the character. I think her honesty about it means she takes it seriously. We … don't really have a way of fully knowing if our patients are truthful, do we?" Miranda asks.

The five of them, Miranda, Laurie King, Gregson Lo, David Swanson, and Jenn Rosenberg nod in unison.

"Truthfully, that sounds more like feeling challenged than a set-up to fail," David offers.

I ask him to continue.

"Being challenged doesn't mean you will automatically fail. Feeling like you're being set up to fail is more manipulative. Is that what you feel is happening?"

I don't. He's absolutely right, and I'm grateful for his observation. I do feel challenged in a way I haven't before. My clients challenge me every day: to reevaluate my skills and self-awareness, to research. They test my limitations.

With Diana, I feel competitively challenged.

There is worry of something greater than dishonesty. Though I am not sure what it is about yet.

I did the thing we are not supposed to do, but some of us do anyway: Googled Diana. She *is* an author, and her books were on the bestsellers' list. She worked as a journalist and had conducted dozens and dozens of interviews, so her request is (or at least seems) legitimate. Working with someone pretending to be something else is, in some form, lying, which makes me question: is her being here about her book truthful?

I have been treading on very thin ice in terms of my *own* truths and lies. More lies seem to come out of my mouth than truths lately and I wonder if I am projecting them onto Diana.

"Are you anxious of turning June into whoever she's acting as, or of failure?"

"A little bit of both. I think the failure could be detrimental to her well-being," I answer Miranda. I don't mean to, but I look at Jenn, who had a patient retaliate and accuse her of poor therapy. Given everything I had heard, the patient was right.

"I know," Jenn says. "It's *her* all over again." She's referring to a former patient, Julia.

"I'm sorry," I take a sip of wine. "That was insensitive of me. I didn't mean to look … I …"

"No. You're right. I even considered leaving the field." She looks down at her wine, non-verbally confessing, *I sho-*

uld.

Jenn is thirty-eight, still a young therapist, and has been practicing for ten years. She is a deeply compassionate and smart woman. She listened to Julia berate her on numerous occasions before Julia ended the therapy. Jenn took every bit of it—even admitting when the patient was right.

Therapists are flawed, too. Jenn confided in us and in her own therapist. So long as she takes care of herself in the therapy room—on her own and with her patients—she will prevail. But sitting with the fact that you have derailed, damaged, or harmed a patient isn't something you get over. You just learn to live with it. She had to, as she has a family, a career, and the next few decades of life to live. But it's always there. And I watch her fight it every week.

I direct attention away from Jenn. "What would you do?" I ask the group. "Seriously … therapist cap off."

"Talk to her about your concerns," Jenn says, ignoring my cap-off request. "See if it will impact your work with her—whatever the work entails."

"I'd keep going," Gregson says, grabbing a handful of crackers. "I'd be intrigued. I am for you. This patient knows the risks, I assume, that come with her request. She's seeking you out for her work. Not therapy. You're smart and capable, and you can stop if you feel uncomfortable. The fact that you're asking us tells me you want to keep going. If you didn't, you would refer her out. It's like we tell our patients: *one session at a time.*"

He's right. And again, the group proves themselves smarter than me.

When I get home about three hours later, I am fatigued again. The cheese and crackers were not enough, so I heat up leftovers. It is past seven, so the girls are fed, bathed, and watching *Frozen* under a blanket while Adam and I sit at the other end of the couch mulling over the day's news. Then, he hits me with something unexpected.

"Move out of New York City?" I shake my head. "No, there's absolutely no way."

"You didn't have any objections when we talked about this a year ago."

"Things have changed," I say plainly.

"Yes. They have. The city's getting worse, more dangerous."

"First, I didn't agree last year. I said I'd be willing to talk about it."

"What's changed, then?"

"Me. I have. I don't want to leave the city. I didn't come all the way from England to live in *New England.*" I smile at my bad joke. Adam does, too. "Look, it's like after nine-eleven. It was bad, and we were all scared, grieving. But the city restored itself. It got back to normal—a different normal, but a normal. And it'll happen again."

I will admit, the crime in the city *has* drastically increased. We are practically in a mental health epidemic, post COVID. But we live in a safe neighborhood and have built a community around us.

"Come on … the city it isn't safe for two little girls. Is it fair for them to suffer just because *you* love it here?" He looks over at the girls and insists the apartment is already getting too crowded for the four of us and our dog, a little Yorkie Jane named after Elsa, currently tucked between the girls.

Another example of Adam thinking he knows what is best for everyone and putting me in a position of feeling like I am an inconsiderate, selfish mum and wife. I know my thinking is a bit of a stretch. I am aware of how tired and ill I'm feeling, but to run away the minute things get a little rough isn't the answer, either.

Moving from London to New York was cathartic for me. Leaving the memories of mum, dad, and Joseph behind to start new and fresh was important. I wasn't running *away* from something, I was running *toward* something—an opportunity, a new life, change—that could potentially be very good for me. And it was, because I made it that way. We have agency over our lives; we can choose how we want to start or end things, what's right for us, our relationships. When people say they "have no control," it usually means they don't want to make the choices that will provide them with control.

Tonight, I make my choice. “The city is just fine,” I say.

Though he isn’t wrong about the size of our apartment. Our flat is a little three bedroom—the girl’s share one for now, which gives us an office.

We live in Turtle Bay, sandwiched between Sutton Place and the United Nations, on Fifty-Third and Second Avenue. From the corner of our living room, we get a small glimpse of the East River. I have no intention of leaving it.

Or the city.

Or Miller.

CHAPTER NINE
MAUREEN

"I wish you'd get out of work early more often," Miller says with his hands around my waist. He pulls me close to him, lips deeply pressing against mine. Warm. Wet. A tinge of spearmint. We meet like a couple who's been separated by war, and we don't know when we're going to see each other again: desperately craving one another; relief and freedom.

After my second session with Diana, her portrayal as Eden, I had two coincidental cancellations—Lora at four and Jeremy at five.

I worked since eight this morning, without a break longer than twenty minutes, which I don't often do, but knowing my day would end at three eased my discomfort. As did seeing Miller.

"I'm just glad I work so close to you," I say in the small pockets of time when our lips are unlocked.

It always takes me less than ten minutes to walk briskly to the apartment in NoHo, a halfway point between us. "The place belongs to a family friend. It's been in his family for years, and with the market now, he doesn't want to sell; he offered the place to me when my wife and I were having problems," he told me, when I asked how a place this amazing—large, spacious, *expensive*—could be without an owner.

Sometimes I fear a client recognizing me outside, or one of the other therapist's I share the building with, but so far no one has come up to me, or mentioned they saw me, *thank god.*

"This week has been a lot." He squeezes me tighter and kisses my neck before saying, "Thank your patients for me."

I laugh. He knows I am a psychologist, but not much more than that. Like with Adam, I never talk about work. Miller kisses me again and puts his hand on the side of my face, his fingers gentle. He rubs his thumb along the peach fuzz near my ear. He unlocks his lips and kisses that same spot, softly moaning. "I want you. I *need* you."

We make our way to the bed, where I lay flat on my back. Still fully clothed, waiting for him to undress me, he stops to look at me. He smiles.

I smile back. "What?" I ask.

"You're so beautiful."

I want to say I'm not. I want to say, *I'm wearing my glasses and look plump.* I'm a mother of two, not as tight or soft as I once was (not that he would know), and my skin is stretched and wide. I'm more circular now. But again, he doesn't know. He only knows me as I am and still finds me beautiful. I smile at that.

He leans on top of me and kisses me. He places one hand under the thin layer of my shirt and cradles my right breast, gentle squeezing my nipple. He unhooks the silver clasp on my trousers and pulls them off. He kisses my chest, between my breasts, and down the center of my stomach. "God, I've missed you," he whispers, lowering himself between my legs.

"Miller…" I moan his name, his tongue teasing me.

He puts his hand under my panties and pushes a finger inside me. "You're already so wet," he breathes. "I've barely touched you."

I smile. "That's because I'm with you," I say.

He moves his fingers out, now softly graze the inside of my thighs; I grab his hands and move him forward; I put my hand inside of his underwear, giving him a hand job before fully sliding them off.

"Wait, let me grab a condom." He reaches over to open the drawer of the nightstand. "We're out. Fuck. I don't have one."

"It's fine. I'm on the pill." I pill him back down.

When we finish, we lie side by side, tucked under the covers, our limbs intertwined. He kisses my nose, and I begin to think he could be in love with me. That we have more than just a sex affair connection. I turn over and ask if he wants to go again, but he says, "Not right now." He is tired and just wants to lie with me. I feel wanted, and it has been so long since I have *felt* wanted, so I snuggle close to him and enjoy the tenderness.

Miller pulls me close to him, spooning me. He notices my trembling and the goosebumps running up and down my body because he asks, "That better?" while running his hand up and down my arms.

"Mhm," I whisper. "Yeah. Better."

He smiles. "I love the way you say 'better' ... *bettah.*"

I purse and lick my lips, smiling slightly. "You know, you don't *have* to do the accent."

"Was it that bad?"

"Well, it wasn't good … I'll just say that."

We laugh. He puts his hand on my cheek and coaxes my head onto his chest. His steady breathing soothes me and play with his thin chest hair.

"I don't want to go home," I confess. "I want to stay here."

"What's going on?"

"Eh. I don't want to ruin our afternoon with my rubbish."

"You won't. What's up?

His *what's up* feels impersonal, like a distant friend, but I answer honestly. "It's just … sometimes, it's hard, after hearing what I hear all day, to go home to an equally unhappy place. It just feels like sadness after sadness, disappointment after disappointment, all the time."

"I see what you mean. That'd drive me crazy too."

His response isn't surprising. Miller has never been much of a talker, at least about himself, or his feelings. I get these small waves in which he does disclose information, but he immediately retreats.

"Well," I say switching the subject back to me, "Like I said, sometimes between work and an unhappy marriage I feel very … trapped."

"But you're not," he says, still rubbing my arms, generating warmth.

"I'm not what?"

"Well, trapped. You can leave," Miller says with finality.

"And go where?"

He shrugs, says nothing, until he readjusts his position, which causes me to move away from him. "I'm just saying … you don't have to stay with him," he says.

"But you don't want me either?"

"I thought that wasn't what either of us wanted?"

He's right. It wasn't. *Isn't.* I have to remind myself. I smile. "You're right," and then I kiss him. "Thank you, and I'm sorry."

I shake my head, shake off any earlier feeling that he—we—might in love. It was the loneliness talking again.

Miller runs his hand through his perfect, slightly wavy and messy hair, attempting to flatten out the top. "Don't be sorry. I get how you're feeling." He leans into me and kisses me in a way that reminds me of exactly why I feel so conflicted. Maybe I'm not happy with this arrangement. Maybe I do want more. I guess I'm smiling as the thought runs through my mind, because he asks, "What's that smile for?"

Feeling my cheeks blush, I look at him, and ask him something random. "When is your birthday?"

"What?" He starts to laugh. "Why?"

"I just want to know."

"January 31st," he says.

"That's strange." I smile, and he kisses me again.

"What?"

"Mine's February 1st. It's like where you end, I begin."

He smiles, and Adam's proposal flashes through my mind.

There's no way I'm moving out of New York City.

CHAPTER TEN
MAUREEN

"Eden," I say to Diana, we have gotten into a habit of starting the sessions with Eden. "I hope you don't mind if I start today's session."

It has been a month of sessions with Diana roleplaying as Eden. We have discussed Eden's traumatic experiences involving each of her husbands—discussed the patterns amongst them—and Diana asked psychiatric-related questions: *What does severe child abuse do to the brain; how does it appear in adulthood; what diagnosis would explain periods of complete blackouts of time and memory; what does domestic abuse look like in terms of habits, behaviors, control, and patterns; what is the resulting emotional toll?*

All these questions inspire many of my own. Who is Diana? And what do I really know about her? I'm curious about the woman behind Eden—*the woman behind Diana.*

Additionally, I want to check in with Diana, see if our

work has been helpful, how she is feeling with the work, and the progress on her research.

"Okay," Diana responds.

"Do you mind if I speak with Diana Steinbeck?"

She smiles, like she is embarrassed, but suspicious. "Yes?"

"We have been speaking as Eden for the last few weeks. Today, I want to check in to see how *you* are doing."

The way Diana speaks as Eden conveys some personal indicators. I can't help but wonder if some of what Diana writes is based on pieces of her life or desires … whether she is subconsciously working through them as Eden. Perhaps a safer way of making sense of what had happened to her. Diana often speaks fragmentally—in great detail around how she envisions Eden, and then cuts to, "Would a victim of domestic violence behave in this way?" or "Would a psychopath …?" I sometimes stop her to circle back.

"It's been very helpful to me, coming here," Diana says, nodding in affirmation.

"I'm glad." I don't say more, looking for more to her answer, but Diana looks out the window and takes a deep breath. I leave her in that space for a couple of minutes.

To bring her back, I ask, "Would you mind if I ask some questions about you?"

Fixated on whatever is outside the window, she doesn't respond for a few seconds. "For work purposes, I'd prefer not to overlap the two." Finally, she looks back at me.

"I understand. However, I am giving grace in allowing for this character play. I hope you will oblige my small request. Maybe just for half of today's session, and then, we can return to Eden. Us therapists have a unique way of transitioning our mind from one patient to another. I think I can do the same for Eden and Diana."

She shrugs and readjusts her position three times. "What would you like to know? My childhood? So, you can ask, 'And how does that make you feel?'" She openly scoffs.

She has either seen some bad TV, or been in poor therapy. "Anything you'd like to share," I say. "Something about Diana."

Her cheeks flush. She crosses one leg over the other and folds her arms on her lap. "Well …" She looks down to the right, almost as if she is trying to create an outline for herself. "I'm from Long Island. Um … my parents are good people, I guess. I don't see them a lot. My mother had me when she was in high school. My biological father didn't want her to have me, but she did anyway. I never met him. My mother remarried and had my youngest sister fourteen years ago. Strange, isn't it? To think I have a sibling who could be the same age as my child."

She pauses there, like it is her first acknowledgment of that fact … like it is a painful one. Then, she swallows hard and reaches for her coffee. It carried the aroma of sweet apples when she first walked in. "I am married," she continues, cup in hand. "To a wonderful man." Her tone here is less confident, but she makes direct eye contact.

I nod and wait for her to continue.

"We met almost two decades ago … we have fun, I guess." Now, she looks down at the carpet below her feet. She removes her shoes, lifts one leg up, and tucks it underneath herself. "We are childless." Her face drops, and she continues staring at the floor as she says, "I am infertile. It's me."

"I'm very sorry to hear that. I can't imagine how difficult that must be for you."

"I lost our last baby, a girl we named Marnie, when I was seven months along."

I feel sick and want to cry. Despite my training in these matters, I find it difficult to find the right words. "I'm so sorry," I manage.

Diana retreats, her gaze back on the window.

"You must still be in a lot of pain and grief," I say, after something close to fifteen minutes passes. Allowing the silence between us to say: *I am here*.

Diana nods. "Her heart just stopped beating. It was as simple as that. I went in for my appointment, and when the technician stepped outside, I knew. I was crying by the time she came back in. I was alone; my husband was at work. So, I sobbed into that technician's arms and hated myself for it." Her voice cracks, and she wipes away the falling tears. "I'm sorry."

"You have nothing to apologize for."

"Do you have children?"

I don't know how helpful it will be for her to know, but I wonder if she is seeking some sort of mother-to-mother contact. I answer truthfully. "Two girls."

"How old are they?"

"Ten and six."

Diana doesn't respond.

"You said, 'I'm infertile … it's me.' I wonder how you feel about that?"

She shrugs. "It's my fault."

"I'm sorry you have to feel that, but I hope you truly know, deep down, you didn't cause your infertility. It isn't your fault."

She is silent again. After a minute, I explore why she hated herself for crying with the technician.

"Because Miller wasn't there," she says so quietly I almost can't hear her. Tears start making their way down her cheek one after the other.

"He let you down."

"He did!" She breaks down, head cupped in her hands, like she has been holding it in for so long. "Ugh," she wipes her eyes again with the sleeve of her pale-pink sweater. "I felt so alone, so let down. But it wasn't his fault. He couldn't have known."

"But sometimes we wish those we love could *just know.*"

Diana lowers her head, nodding gently; she closes her eyes, hands clenched in her lap.

In our silence, something occurs to me.

Miller? I squint, as if doing so would provide me of the answers I'm looking at her for: is Miller … my Miller actually *your* Miller?

She looks up, cheekbones wet with tears, *No.* It can't be. She is sitting before me as vulnerable as ever, so I step back outside of my own head and I say, "What happened then?"

Diana inhales sharply, brushes her fingers through her hair, and looks out the window before back at me. "Well, I was about eight months along at that point, well past the point of a miscarriage, and because the–" she pauses, parting and closing her lips, trying to find words, sucking in deep breaths, "well, uh, stillborn … fetus–" she pauses again, "well, since I was only three weeks from my due date, they told me it was safe to wait until I went into labor on my own. But I couldn't bare it; I had my doctor schedule a cesarean. But I had to wait a week. It was unbearable. Sometimes, my body forgot she had–" she angles her eyes down toward her stomach without moving her head. "Died," she finishes. "There were times when I thought I felt her kick, and we rushed to the hospital where the nurses told me it was common 'in these situations.' Apparently, women can have that same sensation even after they give birth. I reminded them I wouldn't know. Nor would I find out." She pauses again.

"And how were you? How did you feel?" A strange question to ask, but I didn't want to assume anything.

"No words can describe what that was like. I had three weeks left; *she* had three weeks left." She pauses, takes a deep breath and holds it before letting it out. "I felt unsexy, unwomanly. I hated myself and my body. I couldn't write. I just laid in my dark room. I didn't want to feel or look at myself. Miller was angry at everything. He barely slept in our room. I tried to suck his dick just to relieve the tension, keep him happy, but he couldn't stay hard. So, I'd stop. He'd apologize and try to fix it, jerk himself off, until we ended up in a fight. I mean, who could blame him?"

I want to comfort her and assure her that her husband probably still found her sexy, beautiful. That it wasn't her fault. I want to give her a hug. But I fight my natural impulses and take a deep breath instead. I nod and ask, "Do you?"

"Do I what?"

"Blame him?" I ask.

"For what?"

"Not being there for you at your appointment, feeling unwomanly, for not being intimate."

"I don't know. Should I?"

"I don't think it's about should or shouldn't, but rather what you felt. There is no wrong or right here." Diana is silent again. So, I ask, "When was this?"

"Three years ago. I was forty."

"Did you speak to anyone about it? Have you ever been to therapy before? Related or unrelated?"

"I attempted suicide about a month after." She looks down at her palms like she's ashamed. "I was pretty absent." She puts two fingers to her temple and salutes, insinuating her mental state was far gone. "After the caesarean, in the hospital, they referred me to a psychiatrist. They gave us the number for a couple's counselor who specializes in interfertility, child-loss grief, etc. But we didn't go. The pills were too easy, and one morning, I just couldn't take it anymore. But there was a bad snowstorm, and school ended up being cancelled. Miller came home and found me unconscious. He called the paramedics, and I was hospitalized for a few days." She laughs when she is finished.

I note her self-gaslighting herself out of the pain. A combination of self-blame and emptiness. I place my hand over my breaking heart. I kick myself for being a psychologist without the right words, but remind myself that sometimes, the best thing to say is what is in your heart. "I'm sorry for what you went through, and what you're still going through. I'm here."

"I am, too. And thank you. I don't even want to try again. I fear it's too late. We're too old. We've also barely had sex in the past few years. I'm scared to." She uncrosses her legs and shifts position on the couch.

"What are you afraid will happen if you do?"

"I'm scared of getting pregnant again and losing another baby. Marnie was our seventh loss over six years. I would still love, more than anything, to be a mom … but my mind and body are tired. On the other hand, I'm scared of not getting pregnant, being too old. Maybe of the sex not being the same as it was, too."

I wonder if she realizes she has still been crying. Tears stream down her face off and on throughout the conversation, dripping down her neck, over her lip, and onto her blouse. I don't say anything; I think she wants to be seen. She has perhaps subdued herself and is finally at a place where she can grieve. So, I let her.

Diana and I sit in silence. I give her the space just to exist in the sadness. I want to speak more about it, but she's graciously given me more time than I have asked for. "I'm happy to continue talking about this, or we can resume with Eden. Please don't take that as I don't care about you. I am just acknowledging that you have given me the time to get to know you better."

She sniffles and finally wipes her face for the first time with the hem of her blouse. "What else can we say about it?"

"A lot," I assure her. "Would you like the rest of the session, Diana?"

She nods, and I happily take her in.

CHAPTER ELEVEN
MAUREEN

Relinquishing Diana's tragic fertility story from my mind has been a challenge all day, for a plethora of, well, uncomfortable reasons. It isn't the first time I have carried something a client has shared with me for some time. I'm normally able to put it away once I get home, with the intention of revisiting it when appropriate, but not in this case.

Rather, I'm overwhelmed with gratitude for my own children and the love I have for them. When I finally walk through the door, Jane welcomes me with open arms—something I seldom get to experience.

"Mummy!" She runs to me with tears in her eyes. I kneel down on the floor and wrap my arms around her. She smells of fresh lavender and strawberry cream from her shampoo. She lifts her sweater and shows me a bruise that takes up half her belly. Violet, with specks of red. I repeat the colors over and over in my head.

"What happened?" I place my hand over it and gently brush it with my finger. I try not to show my anger or worry as I look into her weeping, green eyes and wipe the tears from her cheeks. "My darling, who hurt you?"

"I fell off the playset." She sniffles and buries her soft face into my shoulder. I had somehow forgotten a child's need for her mother. I pick her up; she is heavier than I remember, and I move us into the living room.

We sit on the couch. She wraps her legs around my waist, squeezing me tight. Her hug is medicine. I look at the bruise a second time, anxious she is withholding the truth. "How bad does it hurt, darling?"

Jane's head is still on my shoulder, and she puts her hand over it, still crying.

"Take a deep breath."

She does, and I follow up. "Does that hurt, when you breathe in?"

She nods.

"Does it hurt when I do this?" I gently press two of her fingers to the side of her bruise, on her ribcage.

She nods again just as Eloise walks in.

"Where's your father?" I ask, suddenly aware of the girls seeming to be alone. I don't see Adam.

"In the potty."

Jane tightens her grip around my neck, and I rub her back, "Mummy's here." I kiss the top of her head.

I look down at Eloise, who is standing with her legs spread. She leans back on her heels, rocking bath and forth. "I didn't mean to do it." She looks down and breaks into tears.

"Did Eloise push you?" I lean Jane backward, so I can look in her eyes. She sniffles and nods slightly before falling back onto my shoulder. "I fell down the slide on my belly."

"How did that happen?" I ask, inadvertently revealing my anger. At that, Eloise falls onto her bum and wails. I reach to pull her up and hug her. It feels nice to have both girls in my arms.

"I was running with Katie, and I pushed her by accident." She continues to cry.

"It's okay, Ellie," Jane says.

"Do you hate me?" Eloise asks me, her brown eyes glistening with tears.

"Of course not, El." I kiss her forehead. "I love you both so much."

When Adam comes out, I lift Jane off of my lap and sit her down on the couch, handing her the remote. "Can I talk to you?" I usher Adam out of the room.

Before the pandemic, we seldom worked at home. But when COVID began, we rearranged on our schedules, shifting appointments so neither of us would have a session at the same time. An office we were not sure we needed turned out to be a necessity, and one we are grateful to have. Our office has a large oak desk supporting two monitors, two matching bookshelves, plants in the corner, a sofa chair, and a black floor lamp with gold detailing on the rim that I brought with me from England. I have carried it with me for the last two decades.

"Why the fuck didn't you tell me about Jane?" I whisper-shout.

"You just got home, Ree."

"You should have texted me. What the fuck?"

"Shhh," he puts his finger over my mouth and closes the door to the office completely. "Don't upset them."

"*Me*?! Her bruise is the size of my fist!" I make a fist. "She could be in serious pain, Adam."

"You told me not to bother you at work. I can't know when you're with a patient. She said it doesn't hurt that badly."

I side-eye him. "Are you bloody *mad*? Jane can barely inhale without pain. She told me it hurts to take a deep breath!"

"Should we take her to a doctor?"

"I don't know, Adam," I slap my thighs in frustration. "We could have talked about this if you had called me. She may have cracked a rib."

"Fuck. I didn't think of that," he rubs the back of his neck and peeks out of the room.

"'Course you didn't. You'd rather make *me* look like the bad parent. Why didn't you text me? I would've seen it between sessions. This is our *child.*"

"Fuck you for that. It's not like you've been very present, Ree. You kidding me right now?"

"Fuck *you* for that! You're trying to punish me by hurting our daughter!"

"Hey! I am not hurting her. She said she wasn't that hurt. And it's not like you haven't punished *me* plenty."

"Oh, for fucks' sake, Adam. There's a huge difference between you and our daughter. And *now* you're bringing that up?"

"It's always up."

I rub my palms over my face, infuriated. "Have you done anything to our girls?" I could barely control the hysteria threatening to overtake my voice.

"Don't you dare!" he raises his voice just as I realize there is no sound emitting from the television in the living room. "You know I'd *never* touch our girls. Nor would I use them to make a point." He waves a finger in my face. "I forgave you," he hisses. "If I wanted to punish you, you'd know it."

Now, the silence is uncomfortable, and it reverberates throughout the apartment. Shit. He's right. And I'm a total arse. "You're right. You're right. I'm sorry, Adam." I pause. "I'm so sorry. I'm just scared."

I start pacing around the office, leaning my arms against the desk and lay my head down on them. I have been too pre-occupied with Miller and my affair, and I am afraid that what has happened *is* actually *my* fault. I have not paid enough attention or spent enough time with my babies as I should. I start to cry, but the space between my nose and arm is very sparse, so I sniffle dramatically.

"Hey," Adam walks over to me and puts his hand on my back, rubbing it, as he leans down over me. "Let's see how to-night goes, and in the morning, I'll take her to City MD and have a doctor check it out." He continues rubbing my back before making his way to the back of my head. "Let's not up-set them, okay? I'm sorry."

I look up and open his arms to embrace him. "I'm so sorry, too. You're right."

Back on the couch, I take both girls in each of my arms and cradle them tightly while they watch *Frozen* (again). I somehow love them even more today. I think I'll even let them sleep in our bed tonight.

Around three in the morning, I wake up with a dry throat. It's unbearably cold, so the heat has made the apartment dry. I try not to wake anyone as I strut into the kitchen. I need a drink.

Or two.

Or three.

In the silence, I think back on what Diana had said earlier today: "Because Miller wasn't there."

Miller.

In the moment, I hadn't fully processed what she had said. I was too consumed with her story to fully *hear*-hear it. I knew that if I did, it might reveal something about me—like that I could be sleeping with *her husband.*

My pulse quickens as I placed both hands on the counter to steady myself. It couldn't be … *he* couldn't be the same Miller. Granted, the name is unique and certainly more commonly known as a last name—but it isn't impossibly unique. *Right*?

I think back over to scenarios Miller has shared about his wife—marital problems, that's all he said. He spent some time in Luke's NoHo apartment when they were dealing with "typical strains" he had said, but nothing he said connects to what Diana told me earlier today, about infertility and really heavy grief.

I look out at the apartment, the pictures of Adam and the girls and I on vacations, toys sprawled out on the floor, Adam's shoe by the front door, and take a sip of my drink.

I wonder if Adam suspects my affair. Then, I wonder if he would care.

During the first few months, guilt was like another partner

in our bed. That is, until I realized that Adam shows zero indication of wanting me, desiring me, so why should I feel guilty? After all, this is what drove me to another man. Yes, I am cheating. No, I am not in the right. But is *he*? I love Adam, but there's a reason for the American expression, "old ball and chain." I feel tied to him, trapped. I feel like everything we do, have done, was to fit some sort of expectation: marriage, sex, children, work.

As his wife, I know all sides of him. He is likeable, and difficult. He doesn't have many friends—there's just his best childhood friend, Rob, and two friends from college, George and Chase. They are all married with their own families and jobs, so he doesn't see them much. He is confident, but secretly insecure. He has a need to be right about everything and starts an argument when he isn't. Subtly. Like when I explain how he's wrong he interrupts and mumbles, "Ah. Yes, right. Right. Right." Not allowing me to finish my thought or point. To him, everything is always good or fine. *No,* I want to say, *sometimes, things are not fine*. A bad day doesn't equal a bad life, but a bad day can still be a bad day. As a therapist, he should know this. And as a therapist, I know I should communicate.

I figure if we want to make it work, we would. Our actions, lack of words, seem to prove otherwise.

Not to mention how sexually unsatisfying he is. Since Miller, I can't remember a time when I didn't have to work hard to achieve pleasure. With two toddlers, I was too tired. When we are intimate, it's like he is making love to someone who isn't me. I began to lose myself.

When I met Miller, I found it again. *Found me again.*

I look out into the quiet, dark apartment. The bookshelves and coatracks appear to take the form of something much darker—gangly, black figures … the shadows of my own doing. The depths of my mind reveal the pieces of myself I do not want to see.

As children, we are terrified of monsters under the bed. As a grown woman, I know there's no such thing, but looking out on the darkened apartment I think *monsters don't live under the bed, they live within us.* And mine seem to be coming out … not only making their presence known, but demanding acknowledgment.

I turn my head back to the empty kitchen, standing on the tips of my toes to look out of the small rectangular window at the dark and quiet city. I watch as a cyclist, a few taxis, and miscellaneous cars glide down the road, white sparkling dots of lights illumining from apartments or street lights in the distance. On the sill of the window rests a small, clay robin that Jane had made in her art class last year.

I should be in bed, hugging and holding my babies. Instead, I look down at the bottle of scotch, think of Miller and

Adam, and pour myself another.

CHAPTER TWELVE
DIANA

I take the long way home, weaving down the streets that surround our apartment. I haven't cried over Marnie in months. Maybe a year, even. I kind of hate that she came up during my session with Dr. Sinclair. I find it difficult to discuss my martial problems and infertility with Miller and my friends, let alone a therapist I'm working with only for research purposes.

Sometimes, when I see a mother and daughter on the street and think of her, my heart aches, but no tears fall. I think I've run out of them. But it sort of was refreshing, even enlightening, to talk about her with someone other than Miller (who yells) or my friends (who say, "Everything happens for a reason"). I understand they mean well, but how could losing a child ever be for a reason?

During my second trimester, I was happy despite the will-it-last anxiety. I hadn't experienced much morning sickness or any terrible symptoms. I took time off from writing, and Miller and I went on a beach vacation. I felt physically and mentally well. Everything looked and felt good. Maybe that should've been a clue. Maybe things were going *too* well. I thought it was finally the time we were meant to be parents. We spent our twenties working hard and our thirties in love. Maybe our story was to be parents in our forties. It might be late for some, but for us, even after our losses, it felt right. Perfect. We were ready to trade in cocktails for sippy cups.

Still, we relished in our upcoming life cautiously. I did not want to over-excite myself. We adopted our cats, Lucy and Ethel, started to turn our small second bedroom into a nursery, and picked out a name after learning we were having a girl. Day by day, we told ourselves. Still, I didn't want to deprive myself of the excitement—that's part of the magic. It was the only pregnancy that had gotten far enough along for us to know the gender, and we couldn't wait. Six months in, we told our friends and family. Well, my and Miller's friends, and Miller's family. I haven't spoken to my mother since Miller and I got married. There is no need, really. We had never had much in common. And then it was exactly what I told Dr. Sinclair: Marnie's heart just stopped beating.

She was healthy. I was healthy. But the look on the technician's face was the same one I had seen half a dozen times. The doctor used all the fancy terms to justify the cause, but the reality was quite simple: it was just fucking shitty. Sometimes, shit happens in life, and there is no acceptable medical justification. The delivery room was eerily quiet. There was no high-pitched cry, or the "We have been waiting for you for our entire life" proclamation when they laid her on my chest. My heart was desperate for it to have been a mistake … for her to be alive. Maybe they had been wrong. But the only sounds were the indistinct murmurs of the medical staff.

"Would you like to see her?" a nurse asked us.

"Not like this," I said, pointing to the sheet over my belly to indicate my inability to sit up. Other nurses appeared at my side, and with their help, I moved into a sitting position.

It might have not been the right choice, but we wanted to see the little person we made. They placed her in my arms, and Miller wrapped his around us both. She had my nose and Miller's round face. We wondered the color of her eyes, imagining she had had one of each of ours: a green and blue. Miller and Me. *Di/Mi.*

We sobbed mostly. We smiled. We whispered apologies to her, blaming ourselves. When they took her away, any hope of happiness went with her. Miller and I lay quietly together in the hospital bed. A few nurses cried and then apologized for doing so—they didn't know, but it comforted me. That day, even New York seemed to weep with us. It rained for days.

***

Miller isn't home when I arrive back to the apartment, and I am grateful. I don't let him see me break anymore. At least I try not to.

The living room is comfortably grey with the setting sun. It looks like it is about to rain. Again, New York City knows how to be there for you. She is magical like that.

Our friends thought was it ridiculous to purchase an apartment with floor-to-ceiling glass windows, but we are on the twelfth floor facing East. We have no threat of peepers, and I absolutely love it. Especially when it rains. It is like a giant hug from the universe. If you think all writers live in the same kind of apartment or house—with towering bookcases, a blazing fireplace in the middle, a wide, white mantel, open books scattered everywhere, vinyl's and typewriters—then you are right. We do. I am proud of our home.

We purchased it following the success of *The Convent*, and I worked hard at making the interior feel like a bit of an escape from the hustle and bustle of the city. It is a spacious three-bedroom, complete with marble countertops and a long, oak dining table with six emerald, velvet chairs surrounding it. The dining area connects to the living room, where we have a soft, beige cloud couch and two vintage chairs.

When you come from a family that doesn't care much for you, you naturally become somewhat of a minimalist. I don't hoard pointless knick-knacks, or "tchotchkes," as Miller calls them, but I do invest time into finding unique pieces during our travels and heirlooms I had hoped to pass down.

I sit on the couch and wrap myself in a blanket, too tired to write. I need a break. I *deserve* a break. I stare out at the lonely city whose brown and silver buildings turn a dark slate gray with the overcast.

"Baby?" I wake to Miller kneeling next to me, his hands on my waist. He's gently rubbing me with his palms, his fingers warm on my skin. I've missed that.

"What time is it?"

"Almost seven."

My body is sore from lying in the same position; I'm not a napper, but I do feel restored. "I'm sorry," I say, realizing I should have prepared dinner. "I can boil some pasta."

"It's okay. I'm glad you're relaxing a little."

I walk to the kitchen and take out a box of rigatoni from the cupboard. "Meat sauce okay?"

He nods.

We are silent for the first few minutes. I watch as the water boils and listen to him change out of his work clothes and wash his face. He returns in gray sweatpants and a black long-sleeved shirt. I look at him, long torso, defined face, damp face—he's beautiful. I smile, but he doesn't reciprocate.

"I miss you," I say with tears in my eyes. *Fuck.*

"I'm here." He walks over and takes me in his arms. "I'm here."

"Are you? You seem so far away. Even now, as you hold me, I can't feel you."

He looks away from me, down at the floor. I know he's unhappy. And that makes me even more unhappy. It has been years since I have felt happy with him, yet I can't imagine life without him.

"I'm here, Di," he says softly. "Always here."

We kiss, and he lifts me onto the counter next to the boiling stove. He puts his hand under my shirt and gently rubs my back with the tips of his fingers. I smile as we kiss again, and more tears leak onto my cheeks. I think I am happy. Or I should be. I put my hand down his sweatpants and stroke his penis. I massage the tip until he stops me. He takes my hand out and places his on top of mine.

"What?"

He steps back, and I spite the comfort of romance.

"What's wrong with me?" I whisper.

"There's nothing wrong with you." He takes my hand and kisses it.

"Then why don't you want me? To touch me?"

"You just said you can't feel me."

It is my fault. That is what he is telling me. And he is right. I can't help but blame myself for where we are. I had put so much pressure on having a baby after we lost our second and third, like I had to prove something to him. Then, it was to keep him, though I never wanted to admit that to anyone. And then, it was to prove something to myself. For the seven months we were pregnant with Marnie, we were happy. Genuinely happy.

I lean my head back as I try not to get angry. I don't want to be angry; I am tired of anger. "I want to," I say.

"But you don't." Miller steps back and stirs the pot.

"You never touch me. You used to. *We used to*, but it's been so long since we've had sex. Passionate sex. Not just we-have-nothing-else-to-do-so-let's-have-sex sex. Or pity sex. And now, when I touch you, you don't want me." I don't know where this is coming from all of the sudden. Maybe it is all the time with Eden, with myself, and with Dr. Sinclair. Maybe it is everything.

Maybe all the things I could not fully feel back then, all the emotions I numbed, are coming out now. I want us to work on things. I don't want to pretend to be okay with him cheating on me anymore. I want to explore what our life can be like with just the two of us, just as it really has always been. We were once happy with it. Maybe this really is all on me.

"I try," he says. He lifts his eyebrow. "The other night?"

"Did you want to? Or were you just horny? There's a difference."

"Jesus. I can't win."

"I'm sorry, Mill, I'm …" I stop. I feel the tears building again.

"What? Please say it."

"I was just thinking of Marnie the other night. That's all." I can't help it. With my little girl's name on my tongue, I begin to cry again.

"Oh, Di, my love. I'm sorry." He takes me in his arms, and I bury myself in his chest. I repeat how sorry I am, and he runs his fingers through the hair resting on my back.

"Why didn't you say anything?"

I shrugged. "I don't know. We haven't talked about her in so long. We haven't talked about much of anything in so long."

He nods.

We're silent again.

"Mill? See?"

"What?" He shrugs. "I don't know what you want me to say."

"Anything! Any. Fucking. Thing. You're not happy. You're tired. You're done!" I shout.

"I've told you I'm happy with our life as it is, Di. Those are your words, not mine. I don't think *you're* happy. I think *you're* tired. I think *you're* done."

"How could you say that?"

"How could you not admit it? You don't want to touch me–"

"*I just tried*!" I scream in his face "*You* took my hand away."

He stands back and sighs, rubbing his chin. I slide off the counter, and when he tries to grab me, I pull away. He says nothing.

I walk to the bathroom and turn on the faucet. Sobbing, I sink down onto the floor beneath me. I lay in the fetal position as my head swells into a headache and my heart crumbles into nothing.

CHAPTER THIRTEEN
DIANA

The rest of the week followed with some tension, and it bothered me more than usual, more than the last few months. I can't imagine it being sexy to have your wife only touch you when she wants, how she wants, and for how long she wants. Still, I resent him for not being happy that I touched him at all. He slept on the couch twice in the last week alone, which is not uncommon. But it doesn't help us get closer. He usually stays up later than me, or so he thinks, but the truth is, I am up for the same amount of time, probably feeling what he is: lonesome.

We went uptown for dinner to a new Italian place he read about in *Zagat*, and it was nice to be surrounded by other couples. I felt fancy, especially when he held the Uber car door open for me after insisting I wait while he ran around to my side. He held his hand out for me as I made my way out of the car and then kept it firm in the center of my back. I felt his touch penetrating through my Burberry coat. It was the first expensive piece I bought for myself when I sold my first book over ten years ago. Surprisingly, it still fits, even though the sleeves feel a little snug at times.

The restaurant was dimly lit, so they handed out mini flashlights to aid in viewing the menu—one of the few places in the city that still uses the polyvinyl type. The appetizers were thirty dollars, and I checked to see if he was sure he wanted to eat there. Not that money was a problem between us, but it seemed odd, considering how the week started.

"I think you deserve this. We deserve this," he said.

I didn't argue or question it; I enjoyed the couple of hours of Diana and Miller … *the* Diana and Miller—*MiDi* as I used to call us, like FiDi (the Financial District)—that we were before. We laughed over funny memories, reminisced about our travels, and even talked about planning a trip next summer. We have been wanting to visit Africa: Zimbabwe, Kenya, Tanzania, and Egypt. He caught me up on some work-related stories and city-wide issues. We even discussed which Netflix series we wanted to catch up on.

We felt *regular* again.

I missed this. Just doing things together, whether dinner or laundry. Taking a walk or snuggling on the couch reading.

When we got home, I was still in my coat and boots when

he walked me to the couch, sat me down, and kneeled next to me. He kissed me, pressing gently into me, and I pulled him toward me. The kiss was long and wet, soft and warm. I massaged the back of his neck and trickled my fingers down his back. I started to take off his shirt.

"Are you sure?"

I smiled and nodded.

"Here?"

"Wherever you are, my love," I said.

There was something freeing about the spontaneity … about not being in the bedroom. He took off his shirt, put both of his hands under my blouse, and lifted it over my head. He groaned when he looked at my breasts covered by my black, lace bra. He cupped them with his hands. "Your breasts are perf … your body is perfect."

I pulled him back in, and he stood, with his lips still attached to mine, to pull down his pants. We continued kissing as he pressed himself into me. I laid down on the couch, and he started to unbutton my slacks.

He slipped his hand down my pants and beneath my panties. "You okay?"

I nodded. "Yeah. Actually, I am."

"We can stop now if you need to."

I pull him closer. "I've never wanted you more than I do right now."

He put a finger inside of me, and then two.

I pulled my slacks and panties completely off, and he nestled his head between my legs, tasting every inch of me until I finished.

Miller moved his face up my body and to my lips again. "You still okay?"

I loved how he was checking in with me with tenderness, not resentment. I softly moaned to let him know to continue.

When we finished, we lay silently for a few minutes. I felt a slight headache coming on, but I chalked it up to the adrenaline. His head rested on my chest, and I stroked his cheek.

"I can go again, if you want to," I whispered.

He looked up, surprised. "Really?"

I didn't want the moment to end … wanting him, wanting sex.

After finishing the second time, it was nearly three in the morning. We had finally made our way to the bedroom and were lying together wrapped in our blankets on the floor. I was on top of him, and he held my hips as I rode him until we came.

"Are you drunk?" he asked me when I collapsed next to him.

I laughed. "No. I only had two glasses of wine."

He leaned on his side and said, "I have something for you! Wait!"

I watched his naked body run into the living room, and he returned with something small and black in his hand. He sat crossed-legged next to me. "I wanted to give you this," Miller said as he handed me a velvet box. It felt like he was going to propose.

"What is this for?"

"I just saw it and thought of you." He shrugged, like he was uncomfortable with the sentiment. It was an apology gift, I could tell, something he hadn't done in years, since he … "I'm sorry for the other nights … both of them." He kissed me, another slow, deep, full kiss. "I'm just worried about you."

"I'm tired of hearing that. I'm tired of people worrying about me, pitying me." He leaned back, away from me, and I quickly clarified. "*I'm* also tired of worrying about me, tired of pitying myself. You know what I mean?"

He nodded. "I've been feeling the same way."

"We're trying to take more care of each other than of ourselves, which affects how we take care of each other. I pity me, so I pity you."

"That makes sense."

"So," I leaned up and smiled, a real smile, and looked into his eyes. I missed that kind of smile. I even missed the days when we didn't want a baby just yet. When we wanted to be just us. Maybe we could find it again. Honestly, truthfully, genuinely. "What are you apologizing for?"

He sat back. "What do you mean? I just told you."

"You said for the past couple of nights. But what about those nights?"

"Jesus, Di."

"You have to know what you're apologizing for. I told you mine: pitying you."

"Is that all?"

No. "No. I'm being honest, here. I'm sorry for feeling like you aren't enough for me on your own … that our life isn't whole and complete without a child."

His chest lowered as he exhaled, slow and long.

"I'm sorry to be so heavy," I said.

He pulled me tight to him, allowing me to sink into his chest. He held me for the first time with comfort, not pity. "You're not heavy. Not ever."

"I love you more than I have been sad over the last few years. It hurts me that I didn't feel like you were enough."

He brushed my hair. "I know it wasn't just about me." He kissed my forehead and reached back for the ring box. "Here, I told you, I want you to have this. Let's start new."

"We can't start new," I laughed. "We have to actually confront the old and then move forward."

My head was starting to pound. I was exhausted, still a bit horny, too. I had been craving this kind of connection and communication for so long, and I wanted to savor it. "I feel like I've let you down. And I know I shouldn't say this, but I don't want to lose you. I don't want to be one of the couples who can't have kids and splits up."

"We're still together, and I'm in my forties. I'm tired. I can be happy with just us two."

"It *has* been just us two."

"Has it? It feels like all the shit that's happened sits at the table with us, lays in bed with us." He stopped, looked down. "But nothing's changed, has it? You say you're okay with it being the two of us, but you still act like you aren't."

Likely in response to my *lack* of response, Miller reached for the ring box.

"Maybe this will change things." He opened it, revealing a beautiful, bright, emerald ring. *Beyond* beautiful. It was a comfortable size, oval cut, with four tiny diamonds on each side of it. It sat on a gold band with a twisted detail at the end of the diamonds. It was effort, I knew it was, but I couldn't take it.

"I'm sorry."

"What do you mean?" His eyes widened, and he looked down as though there might be something other than a ring in the box. "What the fuck?" He shut the box, and it made its tiny thud, almost poetically mirroring our relationship.

"I love it, Miller. I just, I can't accept it. At least not right now."

"I thought you–"

"I know, Mill." I didn't need to say anything more for him to know. He looked pathetically at his hands, like the answers or responses he needed were written there for him. I lifted his chin with my fingers and smiled. I didn't fight the tears. "How could you do it to me? And how could you give me an apology ring when you don't know what you are apologizing for?"

"Christ," he said, backing away. "I was just trying to do something nice for you."

"Miller, I know–"

"I'm not chea–"

I started to laugh and held my hand up. "Just don't even. Give me, your wife, that much respect."

We said nothing else; climbed into bed and let that statement rest between us.

Now, en-route to my next session with Dr. Sinclair, I think about how untruthful I was during our last session. It is the only thing I have thought about the past week, other than Miller. I *had* been in therapy before, in college, twice a week, which lasted for two years.

"What did your mother do?" My therapist had asked me.

"*Nothing.*" I told him. "That's the problem." (Like my character, Eden). I not only had to feel emotions I didn't know were stored up inside of me, but actually discover them there. It was not just my mother, but my father, and their lack of care or support.

Ben had changed so much for me, and I think that's what exacerbated my grief. I was grieving for the parts of me that he helped me build. I might not have had much during my first eighteen years, but I had another fifty ahead of me in which I could.

But that was not for Dr. Sinclair to hear or know.

She doesn't deserve to know.

That is not why I am here.

She starts by asking how my week was. "You disclosed some very personal, hard stuff last week, and I just want to check in," she says.

Today, Dr. Sinclair is wearing a long, brown skirt that almost reaches her ankles. Her boots are black and go past her ankles, so I assume they are thigh high. She is wearing an unflattering black sweater with large, white polka dots on it. She doesn't look very attractive. Her hair appears like she hasn't combed it in three days, and her eyes are low and tired. She has shifted her posture more times than the minutes I have been here; the clock above her desk reads 1:06 pm.

"It wasn't all terrible," I say truthfully. It wasn't. With

minimal detail, I tell her about the spat Miller and I had, our date night, and the days that followed. "… but we found a way back to each other. We always do," I say assuringly.

She clears her throat, a light cough. "I'm glad," she says.

I nod, and then get back to business—to Eden. "What can't I say here, with you?" I ask.

"I'm sorry?"

"What are the legal logistics of what I share?"

I am anxious about getting into the details of my character's murder plan. What exactly would provoke a wife to want to murder her husband, and the psychology behind where that thought begins and how it ends. Uncontrolled impulses and the sort of relief Eden will experience. But I am afraid of going too far, revealing something that could seem potentially threatening … something that Dr. Sinclair will feel uncomfortable about or obligated to report, even role-playing. I don't want her to question the at what point the hypothetical becomes reality.

"Is there something I should be cautious about saying?" I ask. "Something that would concern you?"

"If you were planning on hurting yourself or someone else, that would concern me. I'd have to report it, for your own or someone else's safety." She pauses and then continues. "We have an agreement here. Your character is planning on murdering her husband and his girlfriend …"

I nod.

"How will I trust you?" I ask.

"How will I trust you?" she returns. Then she softens her face and continues. "You asked for my expertise on psychopaths and their pathology …"

"I'd like to break down a bit of the psychology of vengeance," I say, interrupting her.

She nods. "Okay. Revenge."

"*Vengeance.*" I clarify.

She stiffens her posture. "Vengeance."

"Do you think there are any cases where vengeance is appropriate?"

"It's a valid emotion, so long as it isn't …"

"Murderous in real life. I get it."

She nods.

"Would you say my character is right for seeking vengeance?" I ask.

She nods. "I might validate her feelings."

"So, you validate mine?"

"Mine … as in Eden's? You're Eden, right?"

I laugh and nod. "Of course. Eden's."

PART TWO

CHAPTER ONE
DIANA

It has been two months since my sessions with Dr. Sinclair began, and I'm starting to feel rattled.

I have been gathering information about psychopaths and serial killers, their psychology, and jotting them down in my journal, like the detail-oriented author I hope to appear as. Dr. Sinclair has been patient throughout the process. For every question, she has a detailed answer. Her knowledge and expertise are admirable, I must admit.

Female serial killers don't hunt—they usually kill someone they know, out of revenge or for financial gain; males have a higher percentage rate of killing someone they don't know ... of enjoying the hunt; percentage rates show women who kill their husbands tend to do so in self-defense, or to protect a child; the act of killing one's spouse actually has a word, a noun: matricide.

I have had enough time and sessions as my character Eden Lowell that even *I* am beginning to believe I am Eden, as Dr. Sinclair allows me to.

I am even starting to believe I am actually writing a novel. Eden's story.

MY story.

The apartment is quiet with Miller out—I mean, it's quiet when he is home, too—but at least grief and guilt don't cancer my mind when he is gone. I don't see everything we have lost, like I do when he is home and I look him in the eyes.

His absence gives me plenty of time to focus on writing. Working with Dr. Sinclair has brought a lot of old feelings up, pains from my childhood. Made them feel present, as if events from the past are happening now.

My parents—my mother and stepfather—didn't abuse me, so when people ask why I do not call or visit them, it makes for an awkward conversation. My best friends know why. Miller knows why. But to new people, I say, "You know how things changed with COVID." COVID—if anything, provided plenty of good excuses. *Sorry I can't make it; I feel sick, and I want to make sure it's not COVID. I'm wearing a face mask to protect my health (but really, it's to hide an acne break-out). I haven't had time for a gym membership since getting back out after COVID (when really, I don't want to work out).*

And the list goes on.

For as long as I can remember, my mother ignored me. Plain and simple. She fed me, clothed me, and bathed me, but only until I was grown enough to do it myself. Six, I think. Maybe seven years old. When she married my stepfather, George, she was even less interested in me. And when they had children when I was a pre-teen, I was practically invisible … until they needed a babysitter. The therapist I had in college explained to me they had emotionally neglected me. That just because I had a roof over my head, food, and warm clothes, it didn't mean I wasn't neglected. Children and adolescents need more than that. They need positive affirmations, words of encouragement, and physical touch—being held and hug-ged. "You suffered from emotional malnutrition," she said.

I thought it was a load of bull. I thought, *every teen and young adult is depressed.* I hadn't meant to end my life—the reason I began therapy, after being hospitalized—but I also don't know what I meant to do when I cut my wrists. I did not stay in therapy long enough to figure it out. And sometimes, I wonder if that hindered me in my grief recovery and in my marriage … perhaps even in all aspects of my personal life.

You see? I am now entering the place I thought I had locked up. Somehow, despite every attempt to throw away the key, it reappears … opening the slots of my life I would prefer not to see, hear, or feel.

Writing is my alcohol. My pills. My sex and social media.

Miller used to tell me I overworked, but really, writing is an escapism. I work to give myself some space to not hurt. It is a *gift* to myself, not a punishment. It became a quick and effective antidepressant.

Over the past couple of weeks, I have only compiled the notes from my sessions with Dr. Sinclair. Today, I can execute them. But it has to be done just right.

Perfectly.

One little mishap or mistake can throw my entire plan—all of my writing—off. And it isn't anything an editor or agent can fix.

When Miller comes home, the clock tells me it's seven, but I don't believe it. I had started writing at eleven this morning, and somehow, lunch, dinner, and the sun have come and gone. I close my laptop after checking to make sure I have saved the latest version of my document. I take the notebook I use for my notes and lock it in the top drawer of my filing cabinet. I am almost done; the eight hours of work served me well.

As did the last six months.

Since April.

CHAPTER TWO
MAUREEN

The cold wind smacks against even the covered parts of my body as I make my way to the NoHo apartment, where Miller is expecting me.

With just a few of blocks to go, I'm stopped by a deep, lengthy, high-pitched scream. It is a scream that does not say, *I'm startled* or *I fell.* But one that seems to say, *I am caught under a car; I am on fire; I am being slowly killed.* But when I turn, everything seems ordinary. I look up and down Houston; no one is running or shouting, and the nearest sound of an ambulance seems to be a mile away, at least.

Standing at the corner of 4th and Lafayette Street, I watch the hand on the pedestrian sign flicker, counting down the seconds I have until traffic resumes. The confused expression on my face is shared by the other bystanders looking about for the source of the terrible scream, and I'm relieved that I am not the only one who heard it.

Since about April, I have had a hunch I am being followed or watched. I hate how paranoid I have become—and why I need to be paranoid, given my situation. I sometimes hear loud screams, see a shadow following me, have a feeling someone has just been by my office when I first arrive, or that the floor isn't entirely empty when I leave at the end of the day. I'm not naïve or like the dumb people in horror movies, so I shout out, "Is someone there?" and look behind closed doors and hallway walls.

I feel like I am going mad. Mental. I know how it sounds, especially for someone in my field. Sometimes, I think it might be Adam, trailing or watching me. But that would mean he is sneaky and calculated—something he most certainly is not.

I pick up my pace as I walk the remaining blocks to the apartment. I don't notice much in my path, only mentally anticipate how many steps it will take for me to reach the edge of the sidewalk, and if I have enough time to walk across as the red hand is flashing, ticking down the seconds before the cars have the right of way.

Walking up to the flat, the door is slightly ajar. I see Miller pacing around with his finger to his lips. "Hey you," I say. His tense body frightens me. "Everything okay?" He rushes past me, closes the door, and secures the top lock with the chain.

The flat is a very spacious studio, probably eleven-hundred square feet, as an estimate. There could easily be two bed-rooms, one on each side, if Luke wished to build them. The walls are mostly brick, which I love, with large rectangular windows on a slant. Sometimes, Miller and I open them in the middle of the night and listen to the bustling wind, the traffic, and people chattering above us. The kitchen is directly across from the king-sized bed, which I find kind of sexy when we order food or cook something small together—usually naked.

The bathroom is surprisingly spacious. There is a small step down into the shower and a large clawfoot tub, in which Miller and I often lay. The walls are pretty bare besides a couple of paintings, which come off impersonal. There is a bookshelf, but I never care to look to see what titles are on them, and some real plants that I water when we come by. I tend to do most of the cleaning, making sure to wash the sheets each and every time we make love or sleep in them. There is a convenient washer and dryer just left of the toilet.

"When my wife and I were first having problems, Luke offered this spot to me while we were figuring things out. I only came here a couple of nights, though, to give my wife the space she asked for," was all Miller said about how he had access to it.

"Are you okay?" I ask again.

"There you are," he says, nervously. "I've just had the strangest feeling, that's all."

"What kind of feeling?"

"Nothing, just that … I don't know … like someone was following me."

What?! I sort of choke out an inaudible word, sound, before clearing my throat. "Oh?"

"I don't know. It wouldn't be my wife, or … I don't know, I'm just … I'm not sure this is a good idea anymore."

I don't want to let him in on my feelings, especially since he is already having doubts. I need to keep him calm. "What isn't? This? I'm sure it wasn't your wife. I am certain it was nothing."

He stands in front of me, leaning against the wall between the front door and the kitchen, saying nothing.

"Come here," I say. I pull him close to me. He removes his coat and takes off his shoes. Standing in his jeans and cotton, baby-blue sweater, there is a look in his eyes I don't recognize. "I'm here," I say as I press into him.

"You smell so good," he says.

I look at him and smile. "Come on." I take his hand and lead him to the bed. I immediately start undressing.

For some reason, I'm more eager than usual today. He starts by kissing my mouth, then my neck, all the way down my stomach and thighs until he melts between my legs. When I am finished, he slides a condom on and presses inside of me. His warmth radiates through my entire body.

When we have sex, I don't think of anything. *I can't.* But today, with his naked body lying next to mine, I can't help but think of everything. Especially Diana.

Because Miller wasn't there.

Because Miller wasn't there.

Because Miller wasn't there.

Thinking of Diana's words now, I can feel the heat of my secrets lacing themselves on my face, causing me to blush as I attempt to keep a poker face. Was it really a coincidence?

That doesn't sit right with me. Especially now that I know more about Diana's marriage and how much she struggled to have a baby.

When I gave birth to Jane, my first thought was similar to every new mum's, I imagine: what was life like before this? It was physically, emotionally, and spiritually impossible to imagine life without her.

It is my children who breathe life into my own.

Diana must be suffocating.

Miller puts his hand on my right thigh and brushes it lightly with his thumb; my arm is still wrapped around his. He turns over and kisses the same spot he was brushing. "You seem distracted," he says. "You okay?"

I nod and squeeze his hand. "Just tired. Been a long week." I turn and face him, and he smiles at me.

It can't be.

But Miller is such a unique first name.

Looking in his eyes, I'm torn. What if? What if he—the man I have somehow come to care about so much, the man I can't imagine life without—is *the* Miller who wasn't there when Diana lost her child? Is the man married to Diana? Diana, my client, even if just for her research.

How do I—how can I—continue on this path if he is the same man?

Miller leans in to kiss me, erasing my fears and worries. I smile back. With him, I feel safe. I cannot lose him.

Ethically, I can't reveal my clients to him, but I can certainly get Miller to disclose his wife's identity.

For the first couple of months, Miller and I never talked personally about ourselves. The mystery was fun, and it made the sex hotter. To have someone on you, *in you*, who knows nothing about you ... that was part of the thrill. But slowly, as time passed, it became more than just passionate sex followed by a quick exit. We lingered in the apartment, would take a long nap, or order takeout from Chinatown. I started to reveal a little about myself—why I left London, about my job as a therapist, and my unhappy marriage. I even told him about my daughters.

He spoke little of his work as a teacher and barely touched on the guilt he had for cheating on his wife. She's depressed, he'd said. "She lost her sex drive."

In some ways, I envied him. He never spoke ill of their life the way I did about mine and Adam's.

Our affair had gone from sex to escapism to companionship. Now, it feels like a relationship.

"What's running through that beautiful mind of yours?" he asks.

I fake smile to cover my nervousness. I want to ask, *What did you mean when you said, "I don't think this is a good idea anymore"*? I want to ask for clarity, to both hurt and relieve myself. Only I don't. Sometimes, it is best not to know answers to the questions running through your mind. Not knowing is also power, in addition to self-care. I don't want him to say what I think he is going to: that he wants to end our affair.

Miller reaches for his phone and starts scrolling through an article on a website. I let him enjoy it for a few minutes before speaking. "Miller?"

He looks up and turns over on his side. He leans on his arm and brushes my thigh with his other hand, gently squeezing as he moves higher and higher.

"Do you still have sex with your wife?" I ask.

He removes his hand and sits up. He tilts his head and scoffs.

"I'm serious." I insist.

"Why?"

I don't know why, if I'm honest. I shrug. *Maybe jealousy, maybe envy, maybe guilt.*

"What the fuck kind of question is that?" His face tenses. "Do you still fuck Adam?"

"It's been a while," I admit. "But of course, I sometimes have to."

Miller laughs. "Why do you have to?"

I think of my earlier conversation with Diana, about Eden and having to love her husband. I am starting to see connecti-ons.

"He would suspect something, if I didn't. Does your wife suspect anything?"

"Doubt it," he groans as he stands up. I look at the birth mark on his bum, and smile. I'm embarrassed when he turns and sees me. He leans over the bed and kisses me. I pull him down and he lays on top of me as we continue to kiss. It isn't the appropriate time, but I ask again. "*Do* you?"

He sighs and rolls onto his back, finally succumbing to my question. "I told you a little about her depression, right? Well, she can't have kids. That's taken a toll on her, and … well ..."

I bite my lip. *It has to be Diana.* The temperature of my body rises; my mouth fills with saliva; I try to remain calm. "What's her name? I reckon I've never asked."

"What does it matter what her name is? Do you want it to be yours?"

My cheeks flush. "What?"

"Do you want the title of my wife? Is that what you're saying right now? You want to marry me?"

His face was cold. "Please," I laugh, picking up on his resistance. "Half of why I love this, love you, is that we're not married. I can be me." I realize what I had just said, but he doesn't seem to have heard it. He just sighs like he is relieved … a "Me too" sigh.

Then he says, "Her name's Diana."

Despite my previous intuition, I feel my body knit together with adrenaline. I am at a loss for words, and I struggle to keep the panic from my face. What have I done?

It's bad enough to feel like a failure as a wife as I fall in love with another man. But I have also seen Diana's pain firsthand.

Morally, ethically, professionally … I am suddenly aware of all the ways I am failing now. I know the right thing to do; I just don't know how to do it.

Miller interrupts my thoughts—a welcome reprieve. "I feel guilty having sex with her. It's like she's having some sort of release, after so long … like it means something to her. And here I am …" He looks sad, remorseful.

Yes, here he is. And I can't help but feel pleasure around

that fact. I think of *Miller's wife* Diana, not my client Diana. That, despite her better looks and being years younger than me, Miller prefers *me*. Finds *me* sexy. Loves being with *me*.

And I deserve that.

"How do you know she's not cheating on you, too?" I don't know why I ask, but something about how genuinely he speaks, the way his eyes lower, makes me want to protect him, even from himself.

He frowns. "I don't know, I guess." He pauses and shakes his head. "I really don't think she is. She uses sex, I think."

"To keep you?"

"Maybe, I guess," he says, sounding disappointed.

"Why don't you leave her?"

"For you?"

I retreat under the covers. "I told you … I don't need anything more from you than what I have right here." I'd say I'm surprised by my ability to lie so smoothly, but lately I'm rather surprised when I'm *truthful*.

"After everything she has been through, I can't," he says, segueing back into the main conversation.

"You can."

"Would you leave Adam?"

I don't know. Ignoring him, I ask, "Do you … ever feel guilty?"

"Why the fuck would you ask me that?"

I don't know the answer. Noticing the ring on his finger again, I'm infuriated … jealous. Our whole affair feels out in plain sight, reflected back through that symbol of *their* love. Assuming his answer to my guilt question is yes, I ask, "Why do you come here then?"

He throws his phone on the bed like a child. "I thought for the same reason you do."

"Which is …?"

"Why *do you* come here?" he asks. He lays down and takes a deep breath.

I shake my head. "I'm sorry I brought it up." He doesn't do anything to console me, and that makes me nervous. "I'm going to run a bath," I say. We still have a couple of hours to waste.

An hour later, after the tension is lessened, and we get back to ourselves, Miller orders tacos and we eat in bed, TV on, still naked. "Do you want to watch a movie?" I ask flicking through the channels.

"Yeah. Whatever's on is good." We land in the middle of *It's Complicated*. "Should we really be watching that?"

I laugh. "Probably not."

I lay with my head on his chest, and he rubs my back as he tells me he is happy to be with me.

And despite my earlier protestations, I can no longer deny it: I'm in love.

So in love. And I don't think I can let him go.

I sit up and take his left hand in mine.

"Why do you have your wedding ring on?" I blurt, fully aware I am about to ruin the comfortable moment we had been enjoying. For some reason, I cannot help myself. It feels instinctual, unintentional, like if you found yourself running toward a young child walking into the road, oblivious to an oncoming truck. But come to think of it, he's always worn his ring. It's just that now, the stakes feel higher. It feels like he's still holding on to a bit of Diana when he is with me; and if he does that, how will he know he wants to be with me?

"I haven't really thought about it, I guess." He stares at the ring, like he is re-contemplating everything I have asked him to think about.

I'm embarrassed, then, to have removed my own. Like it is routine for me, the bad wife and even worse human.

Miller moves to take his off. "You don't have to." I reach for his wrist. "I'm sorry."

"Nah, you're right."

He places the ring on the side table and is silent, like he instantly regrets what he just did.

CHAPTER THREE
MAUREEN

"Don't forget, you're bringing the girls to school today," Adam says, soaking wet and stark naked.

I do a double take as I open my eyes. I am in my bedroom. I am not with Miller. Despite their shared masculine appeara-nce, the two men are completely different.

There is a bright-yellow color spilling out of the bathroom, and the steam from the shower and scent of his sandalwood body wash fill the air around me. "Huh?" I lean over the bed and reach for my phone. It is not even five in the morning. "What are you talking about?"

"I told you … I have that conference in Brooklyn at seven."

"Fuck," I sit up. He did tell me. The calendar in my phone even says, Adam conference, Dumbo BK, 7am.

"Well, okay. My alarm was set for seven, you know. You

didn't need to wake me."

"Today's an assembly. They need to be at school by 7:45. So they need to be dressed, fed …"

"Oh, bollocks, Adam, I'm their mother. Not a babysitter. I know what they need. I just didn't know there was an assembly. They'll be ready. I'll wake them at six-thirty." I sit up. "What are ten-and six-year-old's *assembling* about, anyway?"

"It's 'stranger danger,' Ree." He puts air quotes around the phrase. "It's important, so they don't …"

"Okay. Okay. Okay. You didn't need to make this an argument."

He comes over, a towel now wrapped around his waist, still dripping all over the carpet, to my side of the bed. He kisses me, but it feels wrong, like a stranger's kiss: awkward, different, and new. "I didn't know this was an argument." He sits next to me and continues kissing me, a deep, pressing kiss, full of intent.

"Sorry." I lean back. I don't want to kiss him. I think he knows that.

He sighs. "Are we not going to talk about the fact that we haven't had sex since Labor Day?"

I think it was before then. *I hate that we are keeping score.*

Later, in my office, I go over the conversation—or, rather,

lack thereof—with Adam. I hadn't responded to his question. Instead, I complained of a headache, to which he sighed with confirmation, and left for his meeting.

Adam leads me to Miller, which brings me some relief, which brings me to my last session of the day: Diana.

Diana—shit.

Whose husband I'm sleeping with Diana; whose book I'm supposedly a reference for Diana; whose painful infertility story I sat in with her Diana; WHOSE HUSBAND I AM SLEEPING WITH DIANA.

How the fuck am I supposed to face her knowing all that I do? How am I to sit across from her *knowing* that I am part of the reason of her marital troubles?

She doesn't know that, but isn't there some kind of basic human right I possess that wills me to feel responsible and liable for the pain she must be feeling? I can't know for sure if she suspects Miller is having an affair—I can say for sure she can't suspect it is I that he is having the affair with—but I know their marriage isn't happy. He's feeling it, and so must she.

The trepidation plagues my body.

Still, I must be fully present for the clients I have before her.

Thankfully, today is a relatively short day: Claire, Elisabeth, Sean, and Louisa.

When the clock reaches to one, I walk out into the waiting room. "Hi, Diana. Come in," I say. She is wearing a black tracksuit and white trainers. She has a black designer bag—something expensive I'm sure—strapped over her shoulder, and her blonde hair is fixed in two short French braids.

She looks good—healthy and vibrant.

Diana is the sort of woman who doesn't need to put a lot of effort into her appearance. Everything seems to work for her. Her eyes are a tropical blue, almost like glass, hollow nests where not just a child should lay, but where she herself should be found. She normally wears different kinds of jumpers, crème colors, over-sized, long, short, with a vest or trench coat on top, with either leggings, trousers, or denim jeans. She is sleek and stylish, as if she isn't trying at all.

But I do know that all she is trying to do is hold it together.

My judgement takes over, overriding any guilt I struggle with. On the surface, she seems to have the "perfect" life: she is married, a beautiful woman with a successful career, and confident swagger living in New York City.

Then again, there aren't exactly "telling" signs about things like infertility, infidelity, and marital troubles.

I can't help but admire how Diana carries herself—that she does carry herself. I desperately want to know more about her, though I do not know why. I have this yearning to help her … in a way that does not require me to give up Miller.

Feeling conflicted is an understatement.

"Sorry," Diana says, sitting on the couch without removing her coat or purse. She was fixated on her phone, like something concerned her.

"No rush. Whenever you're ready."

I sit—more like plop—down into my chair and run my fingers through my hair as I stare at her.

Why would a man like Miller cheat on a woman like Diana with me?

I suppose it is about her celibacy. According to Miller, I am his only consistent source of release. You would never know, looking at her. You would never suspect.

Sitting across from Diana, I'm then reminded of what exactly I am to Miller. How different Miller and Diana are from me and Adam.

"So," she says, taking out the same thin black notebook from her purse she always has, and opening it. I see black marks, scribbles, and side notes covering the pages. Visually, it's pleasing—the sure sign of an author. "Something wrong?"

"No. I'm sorry. I was just admiring your notebook there," I say. "It looks like you've got a lot of great notes. I'm glad I've been helpful."

"Oh," she says. She angles the notebook up, so the notes are no longer visible. "More than you can know. Now, Eden?"

I nod. "Of course."

CHAPTER FOUR
DIANA

I nearly had a heart attack when my notebook fell visible to Dr. Sinclair. *She couldn't have seen what is on the pages, right?* The words would have been upside down to her, and my handwriting it pretty unpleasant. When I think too fast or am tired or depressed, it becomes nearly illegible, even to me.

I mean, the notes aren't *bad*, per se; and I never write her name. I just keep tabs on what she's wearing, what tenses her, what sets her at ease—anything that can give me information about her through our one-sided "professional" relationship. Instead of panicking, I flip the page over to a blank one and draw a long line. I start writing, Research for new novel #4: the psychology of murder types at the top.

I flatten the page with my hand and internally cringe at the small ink smudge on the page. I glance at my hand and see a matching black streak near the edge of my palm. I try to scrub it away with my fingers, using some saliva.

"So, what does a specific type of murder—strangulation, gunshot, suicide staging—reveal about the killer?" I ask, trying to stay on topic.

CHAPTER FIVE
MAUREEN

I take the bus uptown, as I don't feel like walking forty blocks today. As I approach the bus stop, I suspect I'm being foll-owed again.

I wonder if it's her. *Diana.*

My stomach turns like a roast on a spit; my breaths shorten. I find myself paralyzed, paranoid about my surround-ings. The M15 bus stops outside of the Tisch/NYU Langone Hospital, and I think of Robert.

When I was engaged to Adam, I went a bit mental, in the way I had when Mum passed. I was alone my entire life, and as much as I wanted a family, being engaged—being *an adult doing an adult thing like being engaged*—had me feeling tra-pped.

I knew the damage broken families could cause, not just based on my clients' experiences, but my own: my father's death when I was so young and my mother's illness and subsequent death. I was sure I would repeat the cycle. I wanted the comfort of a family with no strings attached.

So … I did that.

With Adam, I became an engaged woman engaging in an affair. With a patient. His name is Robert Merrill, which sounds like the name of a law or brokerage firm. He was forty at the time, and I was thirty.

He was being treated for depression and borderline personality disorder, which is less common amongst males. He exhibited extreme paranoia and drastic changes in his mood (cheerful in one moment and shifting to full-blown rage within a scary few seconds). He was also on the anti-social spectrum, and had two cases of domestic disputes against him.

Throughout our work together, he made small passes at me: telling me how beautiful I am in a particular blouse or how soft my skin looks. He complimented my figure and mentioned how he thought of me over the weekend. Depending on the nature of his comments, I thanked him, or steered the topic back to him, until one day at the end of his session, he leaned in to kiss me.

And I let him.

The affair lasted for three months. When I came to my senses and confessed my engagement and anxieties about it, Robert was rightfully angry. He shouted and accused me of being a whore and of taking advantage of him … something I could not deny. When he left that afternoon, I did not hear from him again for about a month. I worried day and night about him filing a report against me—despite there being no evidence to back up his claim, it still wouldn't look good on my record—until he showed up at my office when I was in session with another patient. I had never been more humiliated or afraid in my life.

"Did you think you could just forget about me?" Robert asked, barging in.

My patient, Madison, looked at me nervously. Robert avoided eye contact with her, as if she wasn't even in the room. I stood from my chair and told him to leave … that he could come back at a more appropriate, scheduled time … but he stomped like a child and mumbled, "No. No. No."

Madison rose to her feet and excused herself. "It's alright. Things happen. I'll call to reschedule." She never did. I emailed her an apology that evening, but did not hear back.

Robert continued shouting, demanding to know why I had called things off. After repeating to him that I was in a vulnerable and horrible position and took advantage of him, he wouldn't hear it. He insisted he was an adult, capable of making his own decisions, all while refusing to acknowledge the ethical relationship between a patient and therapist.

Refusing my request for him to leave, he then took things

to a dangerous level by brandishing a knife with a thick, wooden, carved handle and grabbing me by the neck. I froze—said nothing, did nothing—paralyzed by something much deeper than fear. That *thing* was living and breathing. That *thing* had my life in his hands.

"Robert," I said in a composed tone. "Please put the knife down. I can't talk and give you what you want with a knife to my neck." I barely managed to look down at the blade without it touching the skin at my throat. When I felt the cold metal, a shiver ripped down my spine. He held it there for so long, goosepimples appeared; I felt the sudden urge to pee. A little trickled out as I did my best to hold it in, until my legs felt the warmth of urine and my trousers were soaked.

He started to lower the knife, and I felt a bit better, but it was still far too close for comfort. "Robert, please. I am so sorry, but this isn't the answer. This isn't right."

He said nothing as I stared into his lifeless eyes. Finally, he blinked, ever so slowly, and backed away. "You told me you loved me," he finally whispered.

"I'm sorry I said that," I explained. To be honest, I didn't recall saying it—I doubted I did—but he was the one with the knife. Reclaiming his power.

"You lied to me. You didn't love me. You just wanted me to fuck you."

I remained silent.

"You loved this dick so much, didn't you?" he said. I froze again as he walked toward me. He took my hand and put it over his penis. "You wanted this dick so much for your tight pussy."

"Robert, stop," I said. I tried to move my hand away, but he lifted the knife back to my throat.

"Get down on your knees."

"Robert, please. Let me make this right. Let me help you. This isn't you. This is what I did to you. Please give me the knife."

He pressed it lightly into my throat. I started crying, hyperventilating. I really thought I was going to die. "Get down on your knees," he demanded again.

I got down on my knees.

"Unzip my pants."

I unzipped his pants.

He took his penis in his hands and started moving it back and forth, and when he was hard, he put it against my face. "Put it in your mouth."

I put it in my mouth.

"Suck it."

I sucked it.

"Lick it."

I opened my mouth slightly and licked it.

Tears streamed down my cheeks like broken, running faucets. My pounding chest made every single cell in my body freeze. I felt mechanical. I was sure I had died, *but how can I still be moving*, I questioned. My knees started to burn from the damp pants that were now allowing the carpet to dig into my knees. I could almost feel the marks forming on my skin.

I hoped someone would come into the room. I had even hoped Madison told someone, or maybe another person could over-hear my tiny yelps when he held the knife to my throat, but no one did.

Just as well, I considered. I deserved it.

"Keep going," he said with a softer inflection.

It was silent for a minute. The loudest silence I had ever felt.

"Keep … going … more … that's it … fuck. Right. There. *Fuck.*"

He came. I tasted him in my mouth and fought sickness.

"Swallow it," he said.

I swallowed.

When he eventually tucked himself in, he told me I could stand.

I stood.

"You made me do it," he said. Then, he raised the knife to his own throat and slid it across his throat. He fell back, and his head hit the ground with a thud. I started screaming. The knife fell from his hand, landing at his fingertips. I grabbed the handle of the door and screamed for help. "Please, someone call 911. He's bleeding to death."

I grabbed my cardigan that was lying on my chair and held it over Robert's neck. I didn't know what I was doing, only that I needed to try and stop the bleeding. I pressed gently into his neck, hoping that whatever I was doing would help.

It was an impulse, one I later regretted. Though I hated to admit it, I eventually thought, *I should have let him die.*

Henry Waterford, another therapist who worked on my floor, came running down the hallway and asked what had happened. He looked down and typed into his BlackBerry as, I assumed, he was dialing for the police. He put the phone to his ear, and I re-introduced myself as Dr. Sinclair. "He was suicidal, had a knife, and cut himself," I managed to say.

Henry Waterford repeated the story on the phone, and paramedics soon arrived.

The cut wasn't deep enough to kill him, according to one of the paramedics. They tended to his wound and gently lifted him onto the stretcher. Henry Waterford was questioned by one officer, and I by another. I couldn't hide behind confidentiality, not with Robert's life at risk, and him bleeding out on my floor. I explained to Officer Jensen I was his therapist for several months, but hadn't seen him in a few weeks. He came in, interrupting a session, to threaten me with the knife.

Officer Jensen was petite and scrawny; I was surprised she

was an officer. She looked no more than one hundred pounds, and her arms were twigs. Her voice fluctuated between stern and soft, depending on who she was speaking to—other officers or me. Her stern voice didn't match her puny exterior, but it was believable. "Why didn't he come for a few weeks?" she asked.

I was so distraught from what was happening, I couldn't think of a proper excuse or lie. I just said, "I don't know. Patients stop coming for all kinds of reasons."

"Did he assault you?" Officer Jensen asked.

I looked down at my soaked pants and over to the spot where I had stood. I hadn't noticed the circle the urine had formed beneath me. I sensed Officer Jensen noticed what I was looking at, too, because she turned her head downward and then looked back up at me. "Do you need medical attention?"

I held my hand over my own throat as I thought of what had happened. Hot flashes surged through my body. I was running on autopilot. "He forced me to give him oral sex," I admitted. I watched her eyes change as they shifted back to the wet spot on the floor. I wanted to crawl into a hole and die.

"Alright," she said. "Let's get you to a hospital and run some tests. I'll meet you down there. Is there someone I can call for you?"

All I wanted was to get out of my pants, take a shower, throw up, and lie in bed … next to my beautiful fiancée. I hadn't thought of him until that very moment, and I began to cry. I just wanted Adam. I needed his arms wrapped around me. I couldn't admit this, but in that moment, I felt more shame over the affair than I had ever before. It wasn't just because of who Robert was, but how I'd never even considered Adam—even after I ended things with Robert. I was so preoccupied with my anxieties about being tied down and the possibility of having a family that I hadn't thought of Adam at all. "I'd like to be the one to call my fiancé, if that's alright. I'm afraid he'll be too worried if it doesn't come from me."

"Sure." Just before Officer Jensen walked away, she leaned into me and stared at me with her wide green eyes. "You have nothing to be embarrassed or ashamed of. This isn't your fault."

I couldn't explain to her that, in fact, it was.

When I got to the hospital, I waited until all of the tests were done and questions answered. They insisted on checking if I was pregnant, despite my saying there was no vaginal sex, and administered tests for HIV/AIDs and other STIs. All of them were negative.

I repeated my statement, giving as detailed an account as I could, but leaving out the affair. I pinned the story a patient fantasizing about a relationship with his therapist. It didn't take much for them to buy it, especially after the doctors were able to extract sperm cells from my mouth. Luckily, I hadn't taken a drink of water or anything afterward.

When Adam arrived, he was in tears. He held me and kissed me over and over, and I completely broke down in his arms. I'd never held anyone as hard as I held him onto that day.

Eventually, his sadness turned into rage, though, and he began shouting at the officers. I tried calming him down, but he had nowhere else to project his anger. They were understanding and managed to do what I couldn't.

Officer Jensen drove us home, where I remained for a week straight. I sent my patients an email explaining a family emergency.

I also confessed my affair to Adam. I had to.

"You have destroyed our ethics, Ree. How could you do that to a patient?"

I was beyond shameful. I told him I got everything I deserved that afternoon.

"No. You didn't deserve for your life to be threatened or to be raped ..."

"It was just oral."

He closed his eyes, clenched his jaw, and took a deep breath. "It's still rape, and you didn't deserve that. But you should report yourself to the b-board." With that, he started to cry.

Tears filled my eyes too. "Adam, I can't. It was just three months, and I … I don't want to lose everything. We want a family, right? How will I support them? You?"

"Ree, even if it was just one-time sex, you should report yourself. That *prick* lost everything the minute you got intimate with him."

"I thought you just said it wasn't my fault."

"I said you didn't deserve it. But his behavior and reaction as per *your* behavior, is."

"Honey," my voice was quivering. "Please."

"I'm not going to tell you what to do or do it for you."

"Then please don't make me."

I knew he was ashamed of me—*I* was ashamed of me. And I made everything worse by begging him to keep my secret.

We postponed our wedding. He didn't want to call off the engagement entirely without hearing what had led me to the affair. "I'm also responsible for it," he said. "I must have done something to provoke it in some way. I'm sorry you didn't think you could talk to me about what was going on with you. That's on me."

It wasn't, but it felt nice to have some of the burden lifted off of me. I was anxious for months after Robert's breakdown. It was difficult to sleep, and I took a cab to and from work. I seldom went out, unless with a group of people, or with Adam by my side. He and I got married six months after our initial date, and it took some time to build the trust back up—lots of couples therapy—and a year and a half later, I was pregnant with Jane, and we settled into our new life … leaving our past behind.

I hadn't thought about Robert much during that time, and still hadn't until recently, when I felt like I was being followed. Like tonight.

Waiting for the bus, I ring the hospital. I wait the fifteen minutes I'm told I will be on hold, and then an additional thirty—it keeps me somewhat distracted on my ride home.

"Hi, this is Dr. Holloway. Who am I speaking with?"

"Lora, it's Dr. Sinclair. How are you?"

"Maureen, how are you? We haven't heard from you for … well, it's been a while."

Lora and I met when Robert was first institutionalized. I was less than trusting with everyone at that time … truly worried the whole thing would end in some sort of fatality, one way or another.

"I'm good, good. You know, busy with my daughters and work," I say, then explain I'm calling to follow up on Robert Merrill.

"Dr. Sinclair, we were told you were notified."

"Notified?" I ask passive-aggressively. I had *not* been notified, and it better not be for what the sudden sting in my chest tells me it will be.

"Robert was released almost two years ago."

Two years. "W-what?" I look at the calendar app on my phone: October 20th, 2022. Which means he was released March 19th, 2020.

"Lora, how could you let him go?"

"Dr. Sinclair," her tone is patronizing. "He was with us for nearly six years and had done impeccable work. I don't mean any disrespect to you, of course, but he did much better under the right care and supervision. You know as well as I do that certain pairings, in any kind of relationship, can cause all kinds of triggers. Robert was able to confront the things that he not only suppressed for most of his adult life, but the ones with you, as well, in addition to the transference that came up for him during his work with you. His love for you." I wince at that. "Please understand, I don't think it was *you,* particularly. If it's any consolation, he was extremely regretful. Once he accepted the outcomes of what happened between you, I was impressed when he said, 'I have forgiven myself, which means I don't have to tell Maureen. I can forgive myself by leaving her alone.'"

Tension knots in my stomach. I don't believe that for a second.

"I'm sorry," Lora continued. "But what exactly is this regarding? Has there been an incident?"

"No, no. Nothing like that." I look out the window beside me. I watch children being pushed in their strollers, elderly people moving at a glacial pace supported by canes, bikers whizzing by, and taxies stopping and going. "I've just had this weird feeling … I don't know what it is, exactly. I just wanted to be sure he was still institutionalized, but now …" I couldn't go on without sounding mad.

"Maureen, if we weren't confident in his recovery, we wouldn't allow him out. You know that COVID caused a spike in mental illness and mental health cases. We're more cautious than ever."

And more overwhelmed than ever, I wanted to say. Lora was certainly not the person to confide in about any anxieties, so I thanked her for her time, and she assured me again of Robert's recovery.

I look back out at the dimming city before me. It seems to have grown dark very quickly. Like the light inside of me.

I know I am not innocent; I do not claim to be. I am not a good person. I often ask myself *how I got here*. I'm also unsure how to get out of the mess I have gotten myself into. Worse, I don't know if I necessarily *want* to. I have cheated on my husband three times since we got engaged. I could have ended it with him instead of cheating, sure. But I wanted children and stability. Yet even when I had both, it was not enough.

Sometimes, I wonder what my clients would think if they knew the terrible things I do … how seldom *I* do the very thing I help them to do. But this brings the "Do I want to stop?" question back. And I don't think I do.

I didn't blame Robert Merrill for his actions, no matter how terrible, painful, or scary they were. As bad as it was for me, I imagine it was worse for him: to have this therapist betray his trust and safe space, to take advantage of him, and to become so hurt by it that he nearly endured a psychotic break, resulting in an assault and subsequent institutionalization.

I, on the other hand, am free. *How is that right?*

I think that's why I seek out comfort from someone else. When I am with Miller … when I was with Robert … I am distracted from the emptiness I feel. The deep unhappiness and dark mood I can't seem to shake. It is like I immerse myself in a multiverse where I have the chance to feel something worthwhile. I'm not worthless.

At home, I worry I am not an adequate mother—my actions certainly don't make me a good role model, and I do not know what to tell Jane or Eloise when they grow up.

I am unfaithful to my husband, no matter his role in it.

Like, for example, how instead of listening or comforting me, he immediately dismissed my fears about Robert with plausible reasons that "should" have erased my feelings, but they did not. Instead, it made me isolate myself from him.

Don't get me wrong—hurting him like this brings me no pleasure, but at the same time, I don't want to leave him. At least I didn't … until I met Miller.

Miller feels like the combination of what I miss with Adam and what I crave in a partner. Maybe I can find some way to convince him to be with me. Maybe then, I can have the life I want most and make my amends. Perhaps I can go back into neuroscience, work with psychopaths once again, or even teach. I can do something.

I will do something.

CHAPTER SIX
DIANA

"Hi baby," Miller says when he walks into the apartment. I am in my office working on my computer, but I suspect he doesn't know that, or he would have spoken louder. I can trace his route around the apartment by the echo of his steps: living room first, then down the hall and to my office door. Before I get a chance to answer him, he opens it, and I quickly close my laptop.

In Miller's hand is a bouquet of pink tulips (my favorite) and baby's breath. The same combination he got me each time I told him I was pregnant. They were my favorite combination. Not anymore. He walks over to me and slides the bouquet out of his way, puts his hand behind my ear, and kisses my neck. "Hi, baby," he says again. I am too stunned to respond. I need a moment to process this strange but beautiful moment, while simultaneously trying not to weep. "I've missed your lips," he all but whispers. "Mine were lonely for you."

I smile back. It isn't *exactly* like his old line, but close. "Hi," I say. It is all I can think of.

He pauses, like he's disappointed, but flourishes his hand from behind his back and offers me the bouquet. "I know what this means, and that's why I got them for you. I don't think we should hide from it anymore, you know?"

"*Suuure*," I draw out the word, confused.

"How was your day?"

"Better now," I smile, sit up, and kiss him back. "But seriously, what's going on?"

"I want to work on things with you. I *miss* you. I *really* miss you. I told you after everything that happened that I was happy with our life without children, and I am, but I didn't think to ask if *you* are. And it's okay that you're not. I was so focused on trying to get *back* to the life we had before we ever tried, instead of the life we have now, without one. Those are different things. And that's okay, too. I'm sorry. About the sex, about the closed-off behavior … about everything."

I set the bouquet down on top of my rose-gold MacBook and remember the first time he gave me this exact combination. I had been nauseous for days, throwing up, but every test I took was negative. One afternoon, I *could not* get off the bathroom floor. I was vomiting every two minutes to the second. Somehow, I managed to hoist myself up and pee, when I couldn't hold it any longer. I grabbed one of the pregnancy tests I left under the sink and waited the three minutes until the lines appeared: pregnant. I called Miller at work and yelled into the phone, "I'm pregnant!" I was so happy, I laughed between the episodes of vomiting before finally leaning against the wall, crying, with the stick still in hand. He came home with two bouquets: one of pink tulips and baby's breath for the baby he was sure was a girl, and one of white roses with a single red one, for me. "In a field of roses, I'd always pick you," he said.

The memory pangs my chest.

"Let's go into the living room," I say.

He follows me, taking the bouquet with him and closing the door behind us. We pass through the foyer, turn left, and take a seat across from each other on the couch. I pull a blanket over me for security and take the flowers from his grip. I smell them and smile. "These are lovely. Thank you, babe."

He slips off his Nikes and tosses them to the side, irking me a little bit because he did not take them off at the front door, but when he pulls a leg up over his other on the couch, I am grateful he thought of removing them. I am going to have to open myself up to new perspectives if we're going to work on things: noticing his efforts and keeping from immediately rushing to a negative thought.

"So, what did you mean, we shouldn't hide from it anymore?"

"I'm not saying I want to try again. I'm not saying I don't want to try again, either. But we don't have to live with the elephant in the room anymore. I want you to talk to me about anything … baby-related, or not."

He pauses, like he's waiting for me to divulge three years of grief to him, but I hold my composure.

"I mean, I know they weren't technically *born*, but they were people. Little people."

I laugh at that.

"They were someone to us. And they can still be a part of our lives, even in this form, and we should proudly …"

"Miller … Miller," I interrupt him, knowing I am going to burst into tears any second if he goes on. "Please, please. I don't understand why you're saying this."

"I thought we could always have these flowers in the house. They can't replace our babies or our pain, but they can still be with us this way. I want to work on this new part of our life together."

I don't mean to, but I scoff. "Why? I mean … you can …" I pause.

"No, say it. Please."

"You have no problem getting sex from another woman. If we are *going* to work on us, we have to talk about that."

He tenses, opens his mouth, and then pauses before saying, "Okay."

"You told me it was a one-time thing, and I understood. We hadn't slept with each other in more than a year. I'll be honest; I missed sex, too. I know I didn't talk to you about it—it was such a reminder of what happened, or actually, what didn't happen—and for that, I'm sorry. But I need you to be honest now."

"Okay," he says. "About what, exactly?"

"Why me? I mean, you can go find another woman who can give you everything you want, and whether you decide to have children or not, that's your choice. But why do you want to stay here with me then?" My volume lowers on the last bit.

"I told you. You are my best friend," Miller says. "Because I was hurting, too. Because I would rather never have sex with you for the rest of my life than to have it with someone else."

I close my eyes, holding back any more tears. "I was too forgiving of your cheating. I wouldn't want you to be *okay* with me cheating. I would want you to feel jealous and hurt, and maybe even a little possessive. Don't get me wrong, a part of me did, but not enough. And those emotions are part of why I love you so much."

Miller nods like he understands. Then, he says, "You're right, you know. You can find that stuff anywhere. I can't find you anywhere."

I don't fully believe him. I know what he is capable of. What he has done. What he *is* doing.

"What's so special about me?"

"What *isn't?*"

"I'm serious, babe. I can't go through this with you unless you're completely open and honest."

"I have things to figure out and fix," he says.

We don't say it, but we both know what he means.

Who that means.

CHAPTER SEVEN
DIANA

When a candle is lit, an ember sparks the flame—*an ember becomes the flame.* Grief and rage are the same: you embody it. You become it.

I am anxious to sit with Dr. Sinclair again. I fear I have given too much away; I fear I no longer have control over myself, and that was the very last thing I had. *Control.* I have lost my children. I have lost my marriage. And I have lost myself.

When you lose everything, it happens all at once. I blame myself for staring back at it—watching as my life burning in front of me like fiery embers. There was not a damn thing to do about it, either. Any of it. Not my infertility, my writing, Miller's cheating, or my happiness. The only bright spot in all the darkness is that when you have nothing left, you can't lose anything else.

But with Dr. Sinclair, I stand to gain everything.

I have come this far; the least I can do is finish the work.

I make it a point to be very vanilla. Stick to my superficial script. But I am struggling. The work is becoming repetitive. I have gotten almost everything I need from Dr. Sinclair for my book research: the psychology of domestic violence survivors, their mechanics, alcoholism, how our brains are shaped and changed due to traumatic events … all will provide me the authenticity I strive for to accurately portray these concepts in my book.

The book.

I have almost everything I need … except for what I truly came here for.

The clock tells me I still have half of the session left, but I'm out of questions and propositions.

"You look finished," she says. I tighten up. *She senses it.*

"I don't have any more for you today," I say. "I know we have time left, but I'm just about out of … Eden stuff—" I pause for less than a second before adding, "for now. I'm not ready to cancel our appointments altogether, but if it's okay with you, I'll leave early today."

"It's entirely up to you," she says.

Dr. Sinclair also seems uncomfortable, like the energy has shifted between us. I am halfway between sitting and standing when I sink back into the couch.

I look down and that's when I see it.

"Is everything alright?" she asks.

My body temperature rises. I feel my body flush with heat. "Just a, uh," I pause. "Head rush."

"Take your time," she says as she brushes her hair behind her ear, revealing again a gold ring with an almond-shaped emerald stone nestled between four small diamonds on each side.

The one Miller tried to give me.

Beyond beautiful.

CHAPTER EIGHT
MAUREEN

I just about catch Diana as she collapses near my office door. Her hand is still on the knob as she falls straight down, like the Earth opened up to suck her into it. "Heavens, Diana!" She leans against me with most of her weight. "Diana, are you alright?"

I am down on one knee, and she is kneeling over it. I look at her hand gripping the doorknob before she makes a gurgled cough. I help lean her up. Her eyes look hazy, wet with tears. She closes them tightly and reopens them, partially blinking as she attempts to stand. "Let me call someone for you."

"No," she says. "I'm fine."

"Are you ill? Would you like me to admit you into hospital?"

"I'm not fucking *insane,* and you're not a medical doctor."

She leans over as if she's going to be sick.

"Diana, let me help you."

She puts her hand against the floor for support. "You have done quite enough," she hisses.

I stand silently as I watch her. She's frail and thin—no more than 110 lbs. She looks unsteady and unwell, still like she might be sick, but I say nothing. The most important thing I have learned from my profession, and from those closest to me, is that you cannot help someone who does not want to be helped. If a student doesn't want to pass an exam, she will never open a textbook.

When she is on her feet again, she apologizes. "I don't know what came over me."

"You're feeling better?"

"Oh, I am seeing things much clearer now. For the first time in months … years, really."

I don't know what she means by that, but I do sense an underlying threat. My stomach churns. I feel myself persp-iring: starting from the back of my neck, to beats on my fore-head, under my arms, and down to my palms. I feel almost like Diana: about to collapse, but I don't. The thought imm-ediately screams in my head:

She knows.

CHAPTER NINE
DIANA

For eight months, I have known that Maureen Sinclair is sleeping with my husband. A wife always knows.

I first suspected it around the beginning of the year. Miller had more color in his face, came home at infrequent hours, and made little to no effort to flirt with me, let alone try and sleep with me. I do not know exactly when Maureen began fucking him, but I have been aware of their affair for eight months, three weeks, and four days.

When Miller approached me about wanting to start over again and really work on our relationship, I had only considered Maureen for a split second. I almost told him that I knew who she was. I almost told him about my plan—my plan to kill her, just as Eden would—but if I do, that means I can't carry it out.

Clever, huh? My plan. *My hoax.*

Playing a stupid, naive writer looking to a well-known psychopath expert and therapist for consulting. It was almost too fucking easy. The halfwit sitting across from me, believing I am developing a character I never really planned to write.

Seeing that exquisitely beautiful emerald ring on her bony, wrinkled finger triggered all the rage I had suppressed each and every time I walked into her office.

I know I should be angry at Miller, too, but there is something about Maureen wearing that ring, like she owns him, that makes my blood boil.

When I arrive home, the clock tells me school should be letting out. I wonder if Maureen is going to call him, see him, *fuck him*, or take the smarter approach and stay the hell away from him today.

She could choose any man in the world to go after and have an affair with, and I know for a fact that she has been unfaithful to her husband before, she didn't need to choose Miller. Did she really think that after everything I have been through, I was going to let her—the whore that she is—take my husband?

Did Maureen think she could have two children, a husband, AND Miller?

No fucking way.

CHAPTER TEN
MAUREEN

"When it comes to the psychology of a murderer," Diana begins as we near the end of our session, "is precision, or being meticulous, part of the criteria? Is it part of the thrill?"

I continue working with Diana despite my affair with her husband. If Diana *does* know and has something up her sleeve, it's better to stay close to her. At least, that's what I tell myself through my reddened guilt and obnoxious fear.

At the start of the session, she told me she feels much better now than she did at the end of our last one. "I am prone to fainting," she said, "when my blood sugar gets a little low. I—I guess I had been doing too much running around." She laughs it off as a reoccurring issue that is now under control. I am not so sure if I believe her; after all, she *has* been playing Eden very well, so I know she can put on a pretty convincing act. I can't help but sometimes wonder …

In any case, I speak, with as limited knowledge I have in murderers, about their psychology. Having dealt with many cases of anti-social personality disorder, I have worked with selected patients who had committed more than three killings. While I speak, Diana appears to be taking detailed notes, pausing in-between to look out the window—as she often does when she seems lost in a thought—and then back over to me.

"I've got a lot of great things to go with from here, thank you," she says simply, face devoid of any emotion.

I put my hands on my lap to indicate we have reached the end of our time. Actually, I notice we have gone over by a couple of minutes, so I say, "Seems to me like you must be close to completing your research." I force a smile.

Diana smiles back. "My character is coming along nicely now."

"Of course." I stand and smile as she collects her thin, black notebook, sticks her pen in her black Yves Saint Laurent bag, and shoulders it on her right side. She tosses her hair back into a tight ponytail before putting on her black, wool trench coat.

"I'm sorry to be hasty, but I've got another appointment," I say.

"You don't seem hasty. *I* apologize for keeping you," she says in a patronizing tone.

We are definitely playing a game.

I thought by keeping the research component of our sessions top of mind, we could engage in light banter and speak objectively. But now, I worry that ending our profess-ional relationship—which, in some ways, I desperately want to do—may expose secrets. Many secrets.

I am afraid of losing my children. My husband. I don't think Adam could take another affair—not after what happ-ened with Robert Merrill. And rightfully so. He might even report me for that, all these years later, just out of spite.

I am even more afraid of losing Miller.

I would be left with nothing.

I put two fingers to each of my temples, and take a sharp breath in. To the outside world, New York City is huge, mass-ive. But actually, it's very, very small.

Adam has arranged a get-together tonight with friends and colleagues. I forget what for … football, perhaps? Or just one of his no-reason-and-I-could-care-less dinners.

His friends make little to no effort to get together. They have a group text, and when someone's in town, Adam al-ways initiates it. "I thought I'd invite Steven to go out for dinner with us on Friday, since he has a meeting in the city," he'd say. Or, "Joan and Matt are visiting his folks in New

Haven; let's take a ride there." No one ever comes just to see us. I don't know if Adam simply doesn't care, or if he is blind to the one-sided friendships. He seems to put in more effort with them, our daughters, and his patients than he does with me.

So, why should I feel guilty about sleeping with Miller?

Before I step into the apartment, I can hear the chatter and smell the sweet aroma of warm bread and seasoned vegetables. I groan, hang my head low. I had six patients today and am not in the mood to socialize. I need quiet. I need *out* of my head.

When I open the door, Adam walks over. He has a glass of something in his hand and says, "There she is. How was your day?" He kisses my cheek and offers to take my coat and bag—which he never does. "It was fine. Busy."

Our apartment is an open floor plan. When you walk in, the cozy kitchen is to the right. It's small, but there is enough counter space to prepare meals and a full-sized refrigerator. Instead of an island cart, we have a black, marble, circular round table to the side of the kitchen, adjacent to the living room area. We're old-fashioned in that we don't like to watch television with dinner. We sit as a family at the table to eat—no tablets or other distractions.

I greet and briefly chat with Natalie Thompson, his colleague from the clinic, and her husband Bryan; Louis Perez, another colleague from the clinic, and his husband, Ron; two of our neighbors, Mark and Elizabeth; and Adam's two college friends, Max and Reynaldo.

And, on the sofa, holding Jane in her lap, is Diana Steinbeck, with Miller is sitting beside her.

CHAPTER ELEVEN
DIANA

Yes, I was more than a little surprised to discover that the Maureen Sinclair who worked on West 7th street was married to Adam Sinclair, the psychologist with whom I consulted for *The Convent.* I really didn't put two and two together when I found out my husband was cheating on me with her. I haven't thought about Adam at all in the roughly three years since I had asked for his expertise. Of course, when I began digging into Maureen's life, I stumbled upon the uncomfortable connection … and then decided to use it for my benefit.

Running into Adam outside of Lenox Hill Hospital on First Avenue was quite a coincidence. Well, to him. As for me, it was perfectly deliberate. Seeing his face, I was reminded of the stories he told me about his family: his wife and two young daughters. I hadn't batted an eye then.

Imagine my surprise when Adam invited *us*—me and my

husband—to a dinner party he was having at his apartment to kick off the start of autumn, "even if a little late," he said. "I love entertaining. And I'd love to hear about whatever you're working on these days," he continued.

The idea of being in Maureen's house—surrounded by her friends and family, her two young daughters—was not as appealing as intentionally spooking her was.

Grief can easily become other profound emotions, like anger and rage, both of which I feel deeply as I enter their home and see Maureen's towhead daughters neck and neck on the couch watching a movie. For a split second, I even re-consider my plan. But just as quickly, I determine they will be better off without their mother. From everything I have learned about her, being away from her is their best shot at having a good life. I know from experience—I would have been better off without my mother growing up, too. Sometimes, you can feel far lonelier with people around you than when you're actually alone. And that's what growing up was like for me. I can't imagine Maureen a very doting mother.

Despite their age gap, the girls look like they could be twins. Very well-mannered, they come over to say hello to Miller and myself.

We are last to arrive to the party, other than Maureen.

"Can you do my hair like that?" The youngest asks me. She points to my tight bun, delicately braided.

"If it's alright with your dad," I say warmly.

When one girl wants her hair done, naturally, the second will, too. As I'm securing the bobby pin in Jane's hair to keep the braid intact, I glance up just in time to see Maureen's face drop as she approaches me, her daughter on my lap, and Miller.

CHAPTER TWELVE
MAUREEN

I am frozen in place—stuck—like an ice sculpture left in the snow. I can't think of a single coherent word.

With both hands, Jane eases herself off Diana's lap and runs over to me. "Mummy, look at my hair!" She runs her fingers over the braid.

"It looks beautiful," I manage to whisper, bending down to kiss her forehead.

"Ms. Diana did it for me. Look! I'm like Elsa…" she pauses and scrunches her nose, deep in thought. Then, she takes off. "Daddy … look!"

Eloise scoots herself off the chaise lounge to show me her identically styled hair before joining Jane and Adam in the kitchen.

My gaze is stuck on Miller, and there's nothing I can do to change it. Despite it being a clear giveaway of my utter discomfort, I can't tear my eyes away.

I can tell he is just as uncomfortable—just as stunned, flabbergasted—as I am. The two of us. Standing. With our partners. In my home. He rubs his hands together, brushes behind his head, before putting them in his pocket. He takes hands out again; this jittery behavior is making me anxious. I wonder what Diana makes of his behavior.

He doesn't make eye contact with me, I don't know what I was expecting from him, so I glance over at Diana. And as our eyes meet, I fear my lack of words has revealed everything. I am guilt-struck; I want to break down and apologize, right then and there. Beg for mercy.

"Dr. Sinclair," Diana says as she rises to her feet. "I know this must be a shock. I actually worked with Adam for my last book, *The Convent*. I had no idea he was your husband, though. I admit, your last name never triggered my memory. When I saw your photographs around the apartment, I let Adam know you and I were working together now, as part of my research for my next book. I hope me, us here," she gestures to Miller, "doesn't make you uncomfortable in your home."

While Diana is speaking, it all start making sense. From the start, I knew there was something familiar about her, but I couldn't put my finger on it. I glance at the office Adam and I share, where a copy of Diana's last book sits on the bookshelf surrounded by other titles I have forgotten, too. Adam had proudly gloated that the writer he worked with had a best-selling book. Adam and his patients, anonymously of course, are even included in the acknowledgements.

I close my eyes. *I'm an idiot,* I think. This kind, successful writer who has been grieving her infertility and experience-related marital struggles wants to make sure *I'm* comfortable.

Me. The woman who has been fucking her husband for the past year. *She doesn't know*, I say to myself to calm down. If I repeat that enough, maybe it'll be true.

"Thank you, Diana. This is certainly the ... coincidence of coincidences, I guess."

Diana reaches for Miller's arm as he stands, interlocking her fingers with his. She leans over his back and brushes her fingers through his hair. "This is my husband, Miller Stein-beck. I'm not sure you've met." Her tone is so cool and cava-lier, I figure if she does know about us, she should quit writing and give Meryl Streep a run for her money.

I feel the blood rushing to my cheeks, now fearful that I must look rosy standing before them. Miller eyes finally meet mine, but he quickly looks away.

"We haven't, have we?" I rhetorically say, answering Dia-na's statement. "I don't know where we would have met." I extend my hand to him.

"Nice to meet you," says Miller in a low voice. His hang-dog expression always triggers me to roll my eyes. He couldn't look anymore guilty than if he leaned over and kissed me.

"New York: so big, yet so small, as they say," Diana says.

Shit.

Diana takes a step closer to me. "We can leave if this is uncomfortable for you," she says in a low whisper.

"Well, actually …" I begin just as Adam walks over, Jane on his hip, interrupting me. "I see it's true what they say about it being a small world."

What the fuck is happening?

"Diana mentioned she's consulting with you now on a new book. Isn't that funny, honey?"

"Adam and his patients were so helpful with *The Convent*, and look at it," Diana picks up a copy that I didn't notice was sitting on the coffee table—the very one I assumed to be in the office— and continues. "It's a best-seller!"

Adam smiles proudly. "Alright, baby," he sets Jane down, "go entertain your sister in your bedroom. We'll come and check on you in a bit. You're ten years old now. We're giving you responsibility to look after your sister and behave, okay? You have your snacks, juice, and I hooked up Disney Plus on the laptop. Okay?"

"Daddy!" she says groaning, slightly embarrassed. She runs into her bedroom and shuts the door behind her.

“Well, shall we?” Adam asks, indicating the four of us should return to the other guests who, for the last ten minutes, have remained invisible to me.

Diana follows his lead, oblivious to the fact that I was about to take her up on her offer to leave.

CHAPTER THIRTEEN
DIANA

Aside from the brief introductions when Maureen arrived, I don't speak much to her for the rest of the night. Their friends, neighbors, and Adam's colleagues are actually a delight.

Despite knowing about her affair with my husband, dinner goes smoothly. Comfortably, even. Not once did I catch Miller so much as glimpse at Maureen, unless she was speaking, which wasn't often. I can't say the same for her.

Throughout the entire evening, she continuously looked in his direction, took short glances, before quickly averting her eyes. I wonder the thoughts going through her head, particularly, how she feels about Miller all but ignoring her while being affectionate with me.

We leave the party a little after midnight, both of us a bit more than tipsy. We stumble from our elevator to the door of our apartment. I don't know if it is the competition with Maureen, having been around both her and Miller, or what, but once inside, I'm all over him.

I need him right here, *right now*.

At least there's a small perk of not having children—we can have sex anywhere, any time. I whisper to him, "I want you."

He kisses me hard as we topple over the entryway table and shed our shoes and coats. "Careful," he says, parting his lips from mine. "What's the rush?"

"I don't know. I think it was just nice to be out and … normal, for once. I kind of forgot about a lot, I guess. Didn't you?"

"I guess so," he says. He sounds honest. "You're right, it was nice to be … surrounded … by other … people," he says between kisses. "To forget about our troubles for a while."

"Yeah, so you get it." I remove my sweater and trousers and stand in front of him in my black lace bra and thong. "Come on." I continue to kiss him and help him out of his clothes. I then lead him into the bedroom, a place I usually dread having sex in, but feel excited to now.

We pause for a second, but then, I can't wait any longer. I grip his neck with both hands and pull him down onto me, toppling onto the bed. The lights from the city illuminate our room, a perfect glow of grays and blacks and blues, and I feel him harden against me.

He pauses and unlocks himself, looking lost in thought.

"You okay?" I ask.

"Are you sure *you're* okay? I mean, you, us … now?"

"I know! I'm kind of surprised myself," I smile. "Excited, too." I kiss him again.

He pulls away after a minute, his eyes focused on mine. "That was strange tonight, though, wasn't it?" he asks.

"What?"

"You and Maureen?"

My arousal fades at the mere mention of her. "Baby …" I moan, "You really wanna talk about this *now*?"

"I don't know. I just got the sense you were uncomfortable. I didn't know you knew Adam."

"Yes, you did."

"I didn't know his last name." He leans back.

"So? Who cares? I mentioned him to you probably three years ago, and then, well …" There's no need to continue. He knows what happened next.

"Come on," I continue. "I want you here," I point to the bed. "Here," I point to the floor. "And maybe even all over there!" I point outside of the bedroom.

Miller leans back on the bed, pins my arms above my head, and presses into me. "I'm sorry. I am … I was … I mean, I'm sorry. I didn't mean to stop. I love you for this. I'm so happy right now. I love you so much."

When we're finished, we go again.

When we finish again, Miller's head is lying on my chest, and he traces my left side with his finger. I love when he is vulnerable and lets me hold him. I have almost forgotten the feeling. It isn't easy having your disappointments, your fears, exposed, and we have struggled through that. Now, I can feel us coming together again. Connecting. While we lay together in the dark room, interlaced as one, I listen to the gentle traffic moving outside.

I can't help but think about him and Maureen and how my behavior has driven him to feel the need to hide from me. I am partially responsible. I didn't listen to Miller or his needs. I didn't get help for myself. I didn't make it easy to talk to me. I wasn't a good listener. I used sex to hold him whenever I felt him pull away. Of course, he sought more.

Men crave intimacy and connection as much as women love the physical act of sex, too. Yet there is such a divide, as if men and women don't want *both.*

"I love you so much," I say, kissing his chest. "You're my best friend. I hope you know that." I hold back my tears, wanting to tell him I know about him and Maureen, and that he's been lying to me, and that I don't know if I believe him now. But somehow, I still do. We *are* best friends. We always have been. We've just been lost for a while.

But now, we've found each other again. At least, we're

starting to. And if there's any sign of how far he and Maureen will be from each other now, this is it.

"You're my best friend, too," is all he says.

I extend my arm, brushing the soft hairs along his chest. "And I'm sorry I haven't been … good to you over the past few years, and made you do things that …"

"Please don't apologize," he says, stopping me from saying anything else. He starts to weep, and his voice cracks. "Do anything but apologize."

It's nearly five in the morning when we become too tired to talk anymore. I'm starting to fade. "So," I say, "I need you to do something for me."

"Anything," he says. "You name it."

"I need you to end it." I don't need to elaborate; we both know.

He looks deeply embarrassed and avoids my eyes. "Of course, Di," he says, pausing to give himself time to think over his next response. "I was always going to end it."

"Were you?" He nods assuredly, as if I should take his word. As if *his word* is enough, has always been enough. It isn't.

"I need you to do it here. At the apartment. On Monday."

"Look, Di, I don't think–"

"No, Miller. I need you to just say, 'Yes.'"

He hesitates. "Yes."

"Yes … I …?" I push him.

Lying flat on his back, with his eyes hooked on the black ceiling above us, he simply says, "I will end it with her. But–"

"No buts, Miller."

He rubs his eyes. "She doesn't need to come here, to the house."

"Miller, I need you to do this for me." I sit up and wrap the throw blanket around me to indicate I'm serious.

A long moment of silence stretches between us. Then he says, "Fine. I'll invite her here. Monday."

"Thank you." And I mean it.

"Are you … going to be here?"

"Are you out of your mind? No, of course not. Just make sure she goes into my office."

"Your office? But why–"

"You'll do well not to ask questions," I say before standing, getting into bed, and falling asleep.

CHAPTER FOURTEEN
MAUREEN

"I've got it," I say to Adam from behind, taking a plate out of his hand and rinsing it before putting it in the dishwasher. "Why don't you get to bed? It's after midnight." Not that the time matters. I know he doesn't see patients on Fridays, tomorrow; it really isn't about him. I need him to leave me to my thoughts. He walks behind me and kisses my shoulder. With his hands on my waist, he whispers, "Thank you." I tilt my head back slightly and smile before returning to the chores.

I can't bring myself to discuss the Steinbecks with Adam. I don't want to seem anxious about their presence, or Adam might suspect something. He brings them up, instead, though he says nothing more than I wasn't exactly hospitable. Still, he understands how it must have felt to see Diana in our apartment.

According to Adam, he and Diana ran into one another at

Lenox Hill earlier today. Both were there for unrelated matters, which he didn't specify. It didn't seem overly coincidental to him. Not to me, however—it feels like a warning.

"Anyway, are you sure you've got this?" he asks.

I nod.

"I'm going to bed, then. I'm exhausted." Adam reaches for my hand, and I let him kiss me. "You sure you don't want to come with me? I bet the girls will sleep through the night. Why don't we ..." He pulls me close to him from behind, kissing my neck.

I awkwardly stand there until he's done, saying nothing, allowing him to touch me. When he releases his grip, I say, "I don't want stuff to pile up. I'll be there in a bit." He says nothing as he walks away, and we both know we have been letting things pile up for some time.

The next morning, the familiar feeling of being followed once again strikes me as I make my way from my daughter's school to the subway. I wish I had taken a cab or an Uber, but the M train on 53rd and 5th Avenue is my closest option.

While listening for the downtown train, I notice a man in a large overcoat and hat. Not strange for this time to year, as it has gotten quite cold. But his affect is concerning. He's hunched over, hands in his pockets, head down. He reminds me of the Grim Reaper.

I walk towards the back of the platform—the first and last cars are usually the emptiest—and the man does the same. I hang back, hoping he'll pass me as I scroll through my phone, but he doesn't. He stops, too.

I try to tell myself I am just being paranoid again … that I'm on edge because of Diana and Miller. I take the whole ordeal as a sign to leave him. As much as I want to hold onto him, I now wonder if the man I have fallen for is not actually conducive to an idyllic relationship. Perhaps I have fallen in love with the *idea* of him—of the fantasy we indulge and the attention he gives me—rather than the man who, let's face it, is cheating on his wife.

But things have changed now, in a big—or should I say small—embryonic way.

When the train finally arrives, it's jam-packed, and I consider staying on the platform. The crowd at the front hurries out, emptying half the car, and I jump on. Grim Reaper does the same, and a shock-wave surges through me. He turns and lifts his hoodie, revealing a face I do not recognize.

I inhale a breath of pure relief and nearly topple over as the subway engine revs up and pulls forward. "Pardon," I say to the people around me before leaning against the door and closing my eyes.

As luck would have it, my noon patient, Elisabeth, cancelled fifteen minutes before her designated appointment time. It is my second cancellation this week. I'm almost concerned; autumn and winter are usually the busiest times for therapists. I feel somewhat reassured when I remind myself that Elisabeth has become somewhat of an irregular.

We have been working together for almost three years now, mainly focusing on her grief over losing her mother and alcohol dependency as a means to cope. But over the past couple of months, her sessions have dwindled. I should charge her for them, but I don't. I understand that her sporadic cancellations are her way of controlling our separation on her own terms.

"I wanna go out with my friends instead of come to therapy. Is that bad?" she asked. I wanted to shout, *No! You* shouldn't *want to come!*

Instead I say, "No, not at all—that's progress. It doesn't mean that you can't benefit from more work. But we can talk about fewer sessions, if you'd like."

Before my next patient, Jeremy, I consider calling Diana and discussing whether it is still appropriate for us to continue, but I need more than a morning to sort myself out.

That is, until Jeremy does the unexpected.

He walks in happy, a big grin on his face, and tells me he saw his children over the past weekend after having a productive conversation with his ex-wife. He says he owes it to me. I remind him that it's *his* doing: his work, his words, his patience with his ex-wife. Suddenly, he reaches out to hold my arms and (quite unexpectedly) attempts to kiss me.

"Jeremy, I need you to take a step back, please," I say.

"Okay … but can I just give you a hug, as a thank you?" he asks. His tone is filled with gratitude, and while I normally wouldn't accept—especially after what happened with Robert Merrill—Jeremy speaks with such sincerity, I give in.

"Sure," I say, but as I reach for him, he tries to kiss me again.

"Jeremy, please don't kiss me," I say.

"I've realized that the only way I was able to achieve this was with your help. You are the answer."

"I'm not the answer," I say, his grip on me strong. "I'm merely a vessel for you; *you* are the answer."

"*Come. On.*" His grip tightens. "You can't deny what's been happening between us."

"Why don't we sit back down and discuss it?"

"I'm tired of being away from you," he says, ignoring me. "I think you are tired of being away from me, too."

"Why do you think I'm tired of being away from you?"

"Well, first, the hug." He finally releases his grip. He starts pacing. "You wanted me to work things out with my ex—to be pleasant … but not get back together–"

I shake my head. "I never said–"

"You wanted to hear *all* about my date, the intimate details–"

"Not the details you're implying. You weren't–"

"And I catch you looking at me."

He pauses, finally done with his monologue, and stands with his arms wide open, indicating he would like to embrace me again.

"Please sit, Jeremy," I say, extending a hand toward the patient couch as I move to my chair.

I need to restore order.

I don't know what's happening. I am trying to hide my panic … to push away the thoughts that trigger Robert Merrill, Adam, my daughters, Miller … Diana Steinbeck.

Do I have some sort of sign in my office I'm not privy to that welcomes this behavior? *Am I the sign*?

I don't want to blame anything I have done with Jeremy as a provocation of this kind of behavior. Sensitive to the power of transference, projecting emotions onto a therapist, still, I cannot allow a Robert 2.0 to happen.

Since Robert, I have worked hard to maintain the *do no harm* oath. I'm sure I've done nothing to mentally seduce Jeremy. So, his *I catch you looking at me* catches me very off guard.

Especially since I don't *see* Jeremy in a desirable way; I don't even find him attractive. Of course, I can't say this, but I do say, "I apologize for any look you might have considered suggestive. I do. I'd like to discuss what it feels like for you to share this with me."

He cocks his head, rolling his eyes, like my proposition is preposterous. "Share what?"

"Your feelings, the idea that I look at you."

"You do." He's still standing, and now, he kneels over in front of me. His head is near my knees.

"Robert–"

"Robert?"

Shit. "Jeremy, I … I do apologize, I …"

"Is Robert your husband?"

"Jeremy, I apologize, and–"

He puts a hand on my knee. I push it away. "Jeremy. I'm going to have to ask you to leave. This is inappropriate behavior. I have asked you to sit on the couch, to talk about this, but now, you're not respecting my physical boundaries. I'm happy to refer you to another doctor, so …"

"I don't want another doctor, Maureen. I want you."

"Dr. Sinclair," I remind him. "If you don't leave now, I'm going to call the police. I'm asking you to go." I am not going to make the same mistake twice.

Jeremy stands without saying another word, grabs his keys and wallet from the table closest to the door, and retreats while hissing, "Don't expect me to pay for this." He slams the door behind him.

Less than a minute later, I am heaving my breakfast into the garbage, unable to make it to the bathroom. Frankly, I'm too scared to leave my office. Since I began seeing Miller, and Diana, for that matter, things have been spiraling out of control.

I have been losing control.

I didn't expect a marital affair to come without some drama, but I can't take anymore. If there has ever been a sign for me to take a step away from Miller, from work, to focus on re-aligning my life, this is it.

When I feel well enough, I spend the next half hour calling the rest of my patients for the day and cancelling their appointments. I am too on edge, too impacted by what happened, to attempt to put it aside and focus on work for the next four hours. My patients deserve my undivided attention.

But right now, I need my own undivided attention.

CHAPTER FIFTEEN
MAUREEN

I miss the first twenty minutes of my group meeting. The salad I had for lunch was not sitting well with me, I suppose, because I vomited it back up before finally sucking it back, cat-ching my breath, and calling for an Uber to Miranda's office on 42nd and Sixth Avenue.

I disassociate throughout most of the meeting. Between the nausea and my thoughts about Diana, I am too anxious to lis-ten and too selfish to engage.

Ever since finding out about Diana and Miller, I've seldom slept or eaten. I'm unable to focus when I'm not with a client. It didn't seem too bad until I was at Gristedes food shopping and completely forgot what I had gone for—and how I got there. I had to call Adam for the grocery list.

Had Diana never approached me with her absurd request to collaborate, I would not be in this position. Terminating my work with her might be enough. I could use the party as an example of the conflict of interest—after all, she had worked pretty closely with my husband.

It's more than a little ironic, finding myself in the same position Adam was in when they worked together. She has used us both for research. Though, oddly, I have yet to see her make any progress with her book. I am certainly no expert, and I know little to nothing about the writing or publishing world, but how many more sessions can she possibly spend playing a character she should, retrospectively, be writing?

Maybe she will end it. Then, I wouldn't have to.

Or … *maybe she knows*, I remind myself.

No, I tell myself. *She can't know.*

If she did, there is no way she would continue to work with me, sit across from me, with such modesty and poise.

Toward the end of the group session I have barely contributed to, I say, "Hypothetically, what if a therapist was unknowingly having an affair with a patient's spouse?"

They all pause: Miranda is mid-reach for the bag of crisps; Jenn is opening her iPad; David is pouring a glass of wine for himself and Laurie.

"How … what … *what?"* Miranda asks as if it is a joke.

"It's just hypothetical."

Laurie raises her eyebrow.

"I'm married," I remind her.

"Do you think it's Adam?" Miranda asks. I've confided in her a few times in the past about some marital strains, but not-hing like what she is asking. I feel myself blush. "What!" It comes out more as an explanation than a question. I wince, wishing I had brought the question up to Miranda in private. "No! No! I'm just doing some supervising, and you know, questions come up. I was curious about your thoughts."

"Well, it's obviously highly inappropriate," Jenn says.

"But what if the therapist didn't know?"

"How would she … or he, find out?" David asks.

"Slip of the tongue."

"The patient's?" he asks.

"It would have to be the patient's, right?" Miranda looks at me. I realize there is no other way to ask than to make it look like I am the person in the scenario. "Never mind," I say. "It was hypothetical, anyway."

As the room clears out, I stay until it is just Miranda and me. I start collecting my things: a Chapstick I hadn't used and a hair tie I subconsciously flipped between my fingers over the last hour.

"So," Miranda says, not moving to clear anything, "about the affair question."

My tummy starts to feel queasy again. I pop in a fresh pi-ece of gum to distract my taste buds. I nod. "Mhm …"

"Are you and Adam having troubles again? Are you unhappy?"

I appreciate how forward her questions are, free of judgement.

"Not troubles, really. We're just not connecting right now."

"I'm sorry to hear that, Maureen. It happens, of course, but you have mentioned this a lot over the past few years. I don't want to pressure you into saying anything you don't want to, but I'm here if you want to talk."

"Thank you, Miranda. And it's, I don't know if I would say, *troubling* … no couple is happy *all* the time, even the ones who last fifty years. They have to get through the bad years in order to sustain a lifetime, right?"

"That's true," she says with a less confident tone. "Like I said, I'm here for you as a colleague and as a friend."

"Of course, Miranda. I have long admired and respected you and *do* consider you a friend."

"Good."

I lean in close to her. "Look … it's just hypothetical."

She nods.

"Say a patient said their new partner is Brad Pitt, but *you* are dating Brad Pitt. What would you do?"

"Maureen, if you are sleeping with a patient's husband, whether knowingly or not, and I hope you aren't … you need to end both relationships." Her unprejudiced tone settles my anxiety, but I know I'm also treading on very thin ice. I roll my eyes and sigh.

"I'm not judging your actions," she continues. "What happens in your home is your business, but *if* that is the case, or something close to it, you need to end it."

The feeling of needing to barf comes back; I rush over to the trash can near the door.

"My god, Maureen! Are you alright?" Miranda rushes to my aid. Not much came out, seeing as I already purged most of the salad earlier. "You need to take care of yourself," she says. "Maybe take some time off, rest. I can look after your patients if you need me to. You know you can refer some to me, temporarily."

No. Especially not Diana.

"Thank you, Miranda, but I'm okay. It was just a bad lunch, I promise. Just going to head home and get some sleep. Thank you for listening."

"I'll walk down with you and call you a cab."

As we are waiting, I use all of my energy to hold myself up. My cramping tummy makes me want to lean over like the Hunchback of Notre Dame. I bite my tongue, hoping that causing a new pain will distract the old. I turn to Miranda and speak candidly. "Adam and I are going through a dry spell. A patient said something about a friend who sounded familiar from a couple of years ago; I got anxious. That's all."

"I get it. One time, after three months of sessions, I found out that two of the clients I counseled were exes. One of them showed me an image from a trip, related to a conversation, and I saw it. It seemed like a big coincidence, but the two women lived near my office, so perhaps not so much."

"What happened?"

"I couldn't *tell* either of the women I knew, of course, but then they found out through each other. One of the women wound up leaving. Even if she believed that I could be impartial, she said she needed someone all for herself … someone who could look at her without seeing the other person. Both were gone within a few months, as the other felt similarly. Of course, I didn't say anything. It was very delicate."

"What would you have done if neither found out?"

"What would you have done?" she repeats. "But look, your situation seems like a chance coincidence."

A text alert—the vibrations specifically set for Miller—buzzes a few times, interrupting my thoughts.

Please meet me Monday afternoon at my apartment. Not Luke's. Need to talk to you.

He includes his address.

I wonder if this has to do with the dinner party. I wonder if he's going to end our affair.

I reply: *Need to talk to you, too ... and it isn't about the dinner party.*

Miller: *???*

Me: *We have to do it in person. See you Monday.*

I half-smile, knowing, as Miranda has pointed out, what I have to do.

But I also know I won't.

CHAPTER SIXTEEN
DIANA

Maureen doesn't know that I know. And she won't. At least not until I am ready.

Which will likely be just before her death.

To my knowledge, Miller doesn't know, either. Know that I know Maureen is the women he has been sleeping with.

I am either psychopathic or using my trauma to make jokes, but I cannot help but repeat the famous *Friends* line in my head: *They don't know we know they know we know.*

I think I am probably the only one who can make a murder-related *Friends* reference.

There is no book. Well, there's no book, *per se.* There is certainly no Eden Lowell. Like all of my characters, she came to me for a reason. In this case, to save me. And like all of my characters, a piece of her lives within me.

Eden will die with Maureen.

Last spring, I went to surprise Miller at school. I don't often do that. He works four subway stops from the apartment, near the Trade Center, but I "could use a walk," I told myself. It was lengthy, but like Miller confessed to me the other night, I had hoped to work things out with him.

My biggest obstacle has been sex. I had forgotten what sex without hoping for a result was like. But I was willing to work on it. When I was working on *The Convent*, I considered couples therapy as well as individual therapy to figure out how to not be so triggered during sex.

It was never his fault. But I recognized how I made it so.

I had just about made it to Miller's school when I saw him walking in the opposite direction of the subway, and our apartment, with haste.

He was meeting someone, and I knew it.

They don't know we know they know we know.

I looked down at my phone, and the timestamp read *2:34.* I remember because the numbers were exactly in order. I did not expect to get there so early, but my pace was quickened by adrenaline, my mind clear and inspired, *excited* to try and revive our marriage. It was twenty minutes before school let out, and probably another fifty to sixty before he was due to leave.

Seeing him walking with such purpose froze me in place. I was anxious *my own husband* would see me. And jealous of whatever bitch he was on his way to see. The narrative that we should be angry with our partners, and not with whom they are cheating with, is a load of bull. I am angry at both. Equally. Though the feelings of betrayal, hurt, and disappointment are *all* about Miller, and Miller alone.

As if on autopilot, I followed him to Luke's apartment in NoHo. After already having walked all the way from our apartment, by the time I reached Luke's, I was drenched with sweat, the tears hidden under my sunglasses.

Only vaguely did I know about Miller's access to Luke's apartment. Luke, whose first name is Sam.

My editor, Samuel Luke Schoenberg, was Miller's academic mentor, coincidentally. Sometimes, it made confiding in him harder, and other times, easier … Sam knowing our history. I had only been to Sam's second apartment once or twice, when he was thinking about selling it.

Miller used it when we were having problems, when we needed time apart, just a night or two. I had never thought of it in any other way, for any other reason. Why would I need to?

As Miller sped into the building, I dipped into the Starbucks across the street and planted myself in a seat facing Sam's building for the entire two hours he was inside.

Two hours.

When I said I understood his first infidelity, I meant it. I still do. During the months I was grieving—*we* were grieving—I was not even attempting to play the role of wife. But I never wanted to lose him. The part of me that loved him wanted him to leave, to find a more *conceivable* woman, and have the family he always wanted. I know he would have wanted the same for me, if the roles were reversed. None of that excuses his transgressions, but I understood it, and it made it easier for us to communicate how we felt about it.

Miller confessed his first affair to me—six months after we lost Marnie. He said it was a "one-time thing"—she was a bartender where he was a regular, and it was a release. "But I love you so much, my love. I'm so sorry I hurt you. I was hurting, too, and I didn't know how to talk to you about it, and she was right there, and … I'm sorry I didn't come home and tell you all of the things I should have."

I believed him, because he knows the power of words, and because I wanted to stay with him.

But the second go-around felt different.

As I sat in the Starbucks for two hours, I watched the notification on my phone light up with Miller's text: Urgent school meeting. Some kids acting up again. Be home around 5.

They don't know we know they know we know.

I watched as three people left the building before he did. Two men, and Maureen Sinclair.

I didn't know her name at the time or who she was. My

instinctual reaction when I saw her was he was doing something other than having an affair—I mean, she looked older than me, frumpy and used.

Still, I bought small, cheap cameras on my personal Amazon account and hid them in the corners of the studio apartment using an old key Sam had given us. The same key I assume he uses when meeting Maureen. Taking it out of the drawer again and again like fine habit he had no intention on breaking.

I took the cameras down a week later. And cried every day for weeks.

Following my camera stunt, I shared Miller's phone location with mine when he was in the shower. I have never been one to look through someone else's phone, and I hated who he was turning me into. Locations, following him, secret cameras … What was I doing?

One evening, I followed him to a restaurant in Chelsea and watched how they casually had drinks at the bar, as if they were both unmarried—I saw the ring on her finger. It was like she didn't care—laughing and conversing. In the way I had hoped to again, with *my* husband.

Another time, I followed Maureen after she left Sam's place. I watched her walk the short distance to a tall skyscraper on Seventh Street. On my way home, I Googled it and found that, amongst the many businesses therein, there were psychological services, too. Another quick Google search resul-ted in the therapists' names: Monica Gomez, Henry Waterford, Cynthia Clark, and Maureen Sinclair.

I had her.

Making an appointment to discuss research for my books was the first step. I wasn't sure of another way to meet her wit-hout disclosing who I was. I thought the playacting was a nice touch. I could use some of what I had learned through my reading about killers and psychopaths, their psychology, and how to be slick and deviant …

I was talking to Maureen about Eden planning her hus-band's murder as I was planning hers.

God, I'm a *fucking genius.*

But I am also a hurting, grieving, un-mother and wife.

I'm not quite finished; I still have to play the role of the convincing author.

So, I walk into my next session with Dr. Sinclair with the same intention to spew the same bullshit—the same quest-ions— that I have for the past month and a half.

There is a difference between Eden and myself, however.

Eden will kill again.

After Maureen, I won't.

They don't know we know they know we know.

CHAPTER SEVENTEEN DIANA

Miller and I spent the evening discussing what/how/if our marriage is salvageable. This morning, he headed off to work, and I returned to my office as if nothing happened. Like the world is still normal.

Through and through, we have maintained the romance in our relationship. Our affection and sex life have always been strengths between us … that is, before our stillborn. But since those things were equally important to both of us, it left little room for getting bored with each other. Our schedules were also on our side. Miller would arrive home no later than four-thirty, which meant our nights were wide open—we could go out, cook together, walk through Central Park and across the Brooklyn Bridge, or in Battery Park. We went to museums and then for a drink; if I had a long day of writing, Miller would cook his favorite meal: a well-done steak with roasted potatoes and bread pudding for dessert. On the nights I cooked, I tended to try out different pasta recipes. Pasta is simple, but can be made in so many fashions. I have always had fun with it.

Miller and I enjoyed tabbing the pages of our favorite books of prose that reminded us of the other. I have counted my blessings that I married someone who loves literature more than history or sports. Not that there is anything wrong with those. But he can spark a conversation about the Bronte Sisters and recite Tolstoy by memory.

As many ways as we are similar, we are also so different. I overthink and stress; he is rational. He completely took over everything when we lost Marnie. Not leaving him after cheating on me is a horrible way to say "thank you," but at the time, I didn't know another way to adequately do so.

Triggered by last night's conversation and lost in memories I wish I could subdue, I am too distracted to work. I decide to go on a few forums and discussion groups, to find some comfort there.

My psychiatrist had recommended group therapy—"Group therapy is fabulous," he said, over and over. After observing some sessions myself, I couldn't disagree; but as a participant, a patient, I had little interest. He recommended various grief-processing books and podcasts, as well, and to go online and read other stories from bereaved parents, which would hopefully provide a sense of comradery … of not being totally alone.

And it did. I found that other women also blamed themselves. A very simple but lonely feeling. I also took comfort in their admittance to lack of sex with their partners, too.

Dated just a week ago, there is a discussion involving a woman—Isabella Grace—whose husband cheated on her.

How could you stay with him??!! It's the ultimate betrayal, especially after losing a baby!

I get name-calling and blowout fights. But the minute he fucks another woman, I'm out!

Once a cheater, always a cheater!

The apathy startles me. These are not the kind of comments any grieving mother/victim of cheating wants to hear. All of the exclamation points, the insinuated yelling … where is the empathy?

One comment in particular irks me. It reads: *Do you really think you're so special? Have none of you seen* Gone Girl*?! You aren't the only women in the world who have been cheated on; not to mention, men get cheated on, too. GET SOME SELF-RESPECT. SEE A THERAPIST. LEAVE!*

I laugh out loud at how jaded that commenter is, and then at the idea that it could be written by a cheating asshole himself. I wonder how badly he or she has been hurt.

I am grateful to not have read these kinds of judgmental

comments after my own losses, or when I first found out Miller was cheating on me. Such harsh words directed at someone going through a deeply painful time could have been enough to push me over the edge. Enough to tip the scale for anyone not in the best state of mental health.

Normally, I don't engage in such adolescent behavior by giving these kinds of people exactly what they want: attention. But I can't help it.

I write: *"'Til death do us part." That's a long ass time to be with your husband or wife. I married my husband when I was twenty-seven, and I hope to still be with him at seventy-seven. I can't imagine being with him for more than fifty years and not having gone through some horrible times and mistakes. It isn't what they do, it's how we repair it. As an individual and as a couple. Cheating, yes, is an unforgettable transgression. It does not have to be unforgiveable. We come on here to seek refuge, connection; some of us are mothers who never got to be and may never be; others are mothers grieving the loss of a child. Our marital troubles that come from such tragedy are atypical. Let's be sensitive with one another.*

A platitude, I know. But clichés are traded and hung in tacky shops because they are true. I don't know if my comment is for Isabella, the commenters, or myself, but I believe every word of it. I don't want to believe Miller and I are like these other couples: unsalvageable.

I click out of the forum, my stomach tickled with anxiety, and get back to work.

Miller is planning on bringing Maureen here on Monday, and I need to make sure things are ready. In order to ensure my alibi, should I need one, I continue writing a rough draft of *The Wife I Should Be.*

Some serial killers want to be celebrated, known; a 'hero' and a 'guiding light' to their decedents. Others want to be seen, but not known. They relish in anonymous fame. Hidden in plain sight, some killers—serial or not—sometimes insert themselves into the aftermath of their crime. They may participate in an area search for the victim or attend a vigil. Other killers, usually those close to their victim, may make the death look like an accident via poisoning, slipping an allergy-related spice into their food, or inducing a fatal fall.

For my story, my personal story, I don't want Maureen Sinclair's death to look like an accident. It's going to look intentional.

Very intentional.

CHAPTER EIGHTEEN
MAUREEN

I tried to filter it all out as much as possible—everything that had happened with Jeremy, Diana, Miller—to enjoy what was probably one of the last reasonably warm days in the city with my daughters. Saturday, we went out for pedicures and smoothies. Jane has healed beautifully from her fall, hardly in any pain anymore, so afterward, we walked to the park, where I listened to them happily shriek, laugh, and play: *my* therapy. We picked up two pizzas on the way home: a plain one for the girls and a sausage and pepperoni for Adam and me. We watched *Encanto* (at least it wasn't *Frozen* again), and I let the girls spend more time than usual playing in the bath. They even each got two stories before bed. Sunday, we went out to brunch as a family, then to the Natural History Museum uptown, and finished the afternoon with ice cream. I needed those exact types of reminders of what's really important to regain perspective … to realign myself.

I also needed to admit—to myself—that I am not happy.

I want a divorce.

It took simple pleasures to force myself to just *sit* with myself—feel my emotions and really process what has happened over the last couple of years, rather than just analyze them—because telling yourself what you're feeling isn't the same as *feeling*. At the root of everything, we are more often than not most afraid of sitting with an unwanted emotion over anything else.

Now, I am anxious to be riding the lift up to Miller's apartment. Monday came faster than expected. Funny thing, time. How quickly or how slowly it can go, given one's feelings. A minute can last forever; an hour can feel like the blink of an eye.

The idea of being in the apartment he shares with Diana unsettles me. And why now?

When I reach his door, he opens it with an anxious smile and even more anxious (and awkward) hug. He says Diana is uptown at a meeting with her editor. "I'm meeting her at Serafina for dinner at seven, so we're fine."

Entering their beautifully decorated, *huge* apartment overlooking Lower Manhattan apartment, I am stunned. I wonder if it is even more expensive than Luke's apartment. The way Miller initiated our "relationship," along with how closed off he was, made me assume he was in a horribly trapped, emotionally abusive marriage. But seeing and *knowing* his wife, and now this beautiful apartment, I question his character. Again, I consider the very real possibility that the whole time, I have been falling in love with the *idea* of him.

"You okay?" he asks. I'm staring into the living room, flabbergasted by the beautiful antiques and relics, the paintings on the wall, and the gorgeous bookshelves lined with classics from top to bottom.

"I just … I didn't realize you live in *this* New York City."

Walking slowly into the living room, I'm taking in the book titles, the black marble patterns in the coffee table, and the statue of David's head on a Roman pillar column. The framed pictures on the wall are from various cities and countrysides.

"Those are from our travels," Miller explains. "Poland, Germany, Italy, Indonesia, New Zealand …" he stops mid-sentence, like he is embarrassed or reflecting; I can't tell which.

"D-did you … *take* these?"

"Mhm …" he nods. "Me or Di. We had them edited and blown up, but yeah, we did."

Di.

"Wow," I say, trying to ignore the jealousy and awkwardness between us. "Well, they're beautiful." I walk to the right and extend my finger toward the shot of the Tower Bridge in

London, compelled to trace it.

"Maybe we passed by each other," he says softly. I look at him, standing there in his slacks and olive-green pullover, his hands in his pockets. "In London, I mean," he clarifies with a smile.

I smile back and let the moment sink in.

"I took my daughters to London this past summer, but before then, I hadn't been there since I moved here," I admit. "Twenty or so years ago." I stopped counting.

"Why not?"

"There's nothing left for me in England, I reckon. Mum's gone, friends have moved on … and my family's here." My life in England was harbored with unhappy memories, mistakes, loneliness. Nothing is inviting about England.

"Have you traveled much?" Miller asks, interrupting my thoughts, as unwelcome as they are. The reality is that New York is starting to feel the same as England: a mausoleum containing my infidelities, the people I have hurt, and my own past that I dug a grave for and threw out the shovel.

There isn't much left for me anywhere.

"No, not really," I answer.

Silence settles over us like clouds on a summer beach day, uncomfortably lingering. Our differences hang in the air between us, suddenly overbearing.

Two identical cats with big orange eyes, wide faces, and

thick grey coats come puttering into the room. "Who are these guys?" I ask.

"Lucy and Ethel."

I look up with a cheeky smirk and then back down at them.

"It was my wife's idea," Miller says. "They're British Shorthairs."

I bend down to give Lucy or Ethel, I'm not sure which, a scratch under the chin. I rise back up, and the cats scurry away. Finally, I address the elephant in the room. "So, the other night was interesting."

"God, what the fuck was that?" Miller asks. He starts pacing.

I'm relieved to finally be able to confide in him about it … to know I wasn't the only one suffering through it. "I know, I know. But we're okay," I say. I wrap my arm around him from the back, leaning my chin on his shoulder. "It's alright. Everything is the same. We're okay."

He nods, though his words contradict it. "I don't think so. I really don't. I felt so sorry for my wife. Didn't you feel that way about Adam?"

"Of course," I admit. "I felt like I was sitting in the middle of a lie."

"I felt like I was betraying Di."

Di. Di. Di.

"I mean, you *have* been betraying her. For the past year. It hasn't bothered you before."

He scoffs. "Are you joking? Of course it has! Every time I walk through that fucking door of Sam's—I mean Luke's."

"Did you call me here just to … break up with me, or something?"

"No … I … well–"

"Please, just take some time. You don't have to do anything now. You can have time and space to think."

"I don't think I need it."

I take his hand in mine again, still holding onto hope that he would say what I want to hear, knowing he wouldn't. "Please," I say softly. "Please, it was one dinner." I am surprised to suddenly feel tears in my eyes, as if out of nowhere.

He wraps his arms around me, and I can feel his soft, steady breaths on the top of my head. "I'm sorry. I've hurt you both."

"You haven't hurt me, but you will if you leave me. Please consider *us*." I relax my grip, as does he, but we're still interlocked. "Please think about me. You can't tell me you haven't felt *anything* more than lust over the past year. I know the intimacy isn't one-sided. You felt heard, validated, satisfied with me. You can always have that, with me."

"Maureen, please, don't …"

"There's something I need to talk to you about," I interrupt, not wanting him to finish his thought. "It might change your mind."

The color strips from his face as I feel the blood rushing from mine. We're both thinking the same thing.

"You aren't pregnant. You can't be." It's barely more than a whisper.

"Actually, I can be." I don't admit I had thought it was early menopause. The exhaustion, irritability, sickness … but when I didn't get my period for the second month in a row, I knew better. "I took a pregnancy test," I tell him. "It was positive."

Miller moves to the edge of his bed and sits. We spend thirty minutes in silence as he processes the news. I even start to worry, as he stares at the floor without blinking. "It all makes sense, how I've been feeling physically," I say.

"You're not pregnant," he insists.

"I am," I say. "I've been through it twice before."

"No, you're not." He enunciates each word as he begins pacing back and forth. "Maybe it's Adam's."

"I'm six weeks, Miller. I haven't slept with Adam since Labor Day." I wince. I can't believe I revealed the date.

"Labor Day?" I frown. "What are you going to do?" he asks after several more minutes of silence.

"I'm considering an abortion." He sighs with relief, and I'm immediately offended. "What was that?"

"Nothing. If you think it's the right thing to do …"

"It's not *right.* It's necessary."

"Okay, okay. Look, why don't you see your doctor or something? Get confirmation, to start?"

"No. I don't want to involve anyone else. Not just yet."

"Maybe you're not pregnant. You said you took one test."

"False negatives are way more common than false positives."

"Is that a fact?"

I think about it. "I don't know."

"Look, I'll go out and buy a couple of tests, okay? I'll pay cash, and we'll dispose of them a few blocks down."

"Blimey. I'm not the Queen. It's not that serious."

I can't help but do a bit of snooping around while Miller is out. I've had the itch to do so since we first met, to learn more about him. He's so closed off, I can't help but be curious.

I walk back to the bookshelf: *The Fall* by Albert Camus; *Malcom* by James Purdy; *My Antonia*, *A Lost Lady*, and *Lucy Gayheart* by Willa Cather; *On the Road* by Jack Kerouac. I finally see some that I recognize: *The Brothers Karamazov and The Idiot* by Fyodor Dostoevsky, *Ulysses* by James Joyce, *Invisible Man* by Ralph Ellison, *The Art of Loving* by psychoanalyst Erich Fromm, and *Leaves of Grass*, with it's beautiful, green, hard-cover spine by Walt Whitman. I run my finger along the etching of the leather. Then there is pretty much every book ever written by John Steinbeck, varied in terms of paperback versus hardcover, including *East of Eden*, *Tortilla Flat*, *The Pearl*, *The Winter of Our Discontent*, *The Moon is Down*, *A Russian Journal*, *Cannery Row.* Some look like they could be first editions.

Beautiful titles, I think, wondering if I said it out loud.

There is even a row of small, thin books … plays by Clifford Odets. I never realized Miller is such a serious academic. He is not the plaid-shirt, geeky principal one might envision when hearing his job title.

His apartment, even the bookshelves, are filled with life rather than pieces from Crate & Barrel or Pottery Barn. Everything, even the pictures, is personal.

Theirs.

The silence is looming, like I could scream and not be heard. I wonder if Diana ever feels this way.

I open a copy of *The Winter of Our Discontent* and flip through the first page or two before finding a handwritten note.

For my love. It's just you and me, baby. Always. Or else another light might go out.

Miller

I feel a pinch in my heart as I think about the life they have created together … the one I disrespect every time I am with him. I think of my own life, the children I've brought into it, and Adam.

I have to have the abortion, no matter how guilty I feel or what grief will come with it. Maybe the end of this life will be the catalyst for the end of Miller and me.

At that thought, I start to weep. Then, I completely break down, disgusted with who I have become and everything I have ruined in my life. I can't blame my actions on anything else—not my unhappiness with Adam or the parents who let me down. *They* didn't make the choices I have made in life.

Miller has been gone for twenty minutes. I am a little worried, but collect myself. I am also nervous that Diana's plans might change, and she'll end up walking through the door—*her* door—any minute. I make my way to the front of the apartment and chain-bolt the lock, just in case. *If* she does come home early, I'll have to make up something on the spot.

I move back down the hall toward the bedroom. A glimpse of what looks like an office catches my eye, and I peer inside as I open the door ever so gently.

It's small, more like a large closet than office. There's a beautiful desk against the wall, plants hanging from above it, and a medium-size window on the opposite wall offering a beautiful view of downtown Manhattan. A large, shaggy gray rug covers most of the floor and feels soft and snug under my feet.

I walk over to the desk, curious as to whether there is any hint as to Diana's progress on her new book.

It has always felt so mysterious, despite my being a resource for it.

Documents, a wireless keyboard and mouse, various chargers, and half-empty coffee mugs litter the desktop, but in the middle of it all rests a small, black notebook similar to the one she takes notes in during our sessions. I pick it up gingerly, anxiously, opening it to the first page.

It looks like a diary entry.

CHAPTER NINETEEN
MAUREEN

#1

I don't know how to say "I've fallen in love" without saying those specific words. Yet the truth is, it wasn't so much a "falling" as a "floating." I was lifted into love.

Of course, I'm already married, and so is he ... which makes the whole thing a terribly delicate situation. The few times we've been together, I've noticed how we both keep our wedding bands on. It feels like an homage, or a way to honor our spouses, even while doing what we do.

I release the page from my grip, in shock.

Has she been cheating on Miller? Is this a confession?

I figured Miller was right when he said he seriously doubted she would cheat. I get the sense she isn't the type to do so. I open the page again and continue reading.

We met earlier this month, and I have never felt more like myself; I love myself in a way I never have before. I'm allowed to, now. I've been shown how to.

I've known love many times throughout my lifetime, in many facets. But was I ever this happy? Though I realize it's new, I've never cared for the "honeymoon stage" phrase. How can an actual honeymoon—to celebrate marriage, a unity, a collection of love—be compared to the first few months of a relationship? It can't.

I skip to the bottom, where I see something familiar. My name.

Maureen

xx

I inhale sharply, realizing I have not taken a proper breath since I began reading the page the second time. My fingers are trembling, and beads of sweat dot my forehead as I suddenly realize that somehow, the handwriting even looks like mine.

"What the fuck is this?" I ask out loud.

I flip to another page.

#2

I'm even better in love. I say "better," because it feels more secure. There's more than butterflies inside my stomach. It's a feeling of obsession, and it's building.

I've never felt this way before about any man.

He's not the problem. I think I am. I have him, but I still find myself asking more of him. Is that the problem with all women? Am I just the walking definition of anti-feminism? A woman obsessed with a man so intensely, she'd go to any length to keep him, secure herself with him?

I skip down to the bottom.

I love my husband, but that's all he is. Relationships take work; they require more than just love or connection alone. They require a balance of love, connection, affection, interests, communication, boundaries, support, encouragement, space—and spice. My husband's just a companion. I'd like to think he was once my best friend. And that's what hurts—shouldn't he still be? It's not at all like that with Miller.

Aren't you happy for me, dear reader? Though I know I'm really just talking to myself. But I'd like to think someone else is reading these diary entries.

There is so much going through my mind, one might consider it some type of insanity.

But I know what it really is.

Purity. Authenticity.

Maureen

xx

Flipping through the following pages, I read more of the same: a progression of my affair with Miller, from *my* perspective. I am at a true loss for words as a wave of several different emotions washes through me: anger, confusion, concern … and somehow, empathy.

The worst thought of all then enters my head: she is planning on sending this to Adam or using it to blackmail me. Either of which, I admit, would not be all that outrageous for her to do. If I were in her position, I might do the same. Even worse.

On the other hand, Diana could quite possibly be using this journal technique as a means of processing her emotions. Maybe she's trying to come to an understanding of how her husband has betrayed her.

Every doubt I ever had disappears.

She knows.

Diana clearly knows about the affair. Up until now, I allowed myself to believe she didn't.

But how? And when did she find out? How long has she known?

I flip to the back of the journal and read the last three entries.

#10

I have a new patient, Diana Steinbeck. A writer. What a rubbish career! What good can come from spinning lies for a living? Even worse, she is then credited with literary awards and paid for doing so.

What about the work I do?? Psychology is a real career … work that actually makes an impact.

And what good comes to those who enjoy reading lies during their spare time? I can get on the J.K-Rowling-Harry-Potter bandwagon. I get that. It's clearly fictitious. But some of the rubbish out there can be damaging.

How different is a book from social media? Lies. Lies. Lies. I can't seem to escape all the bloody lies.

Is she really MY Miller's wife??

I mean, they have the same last name, after all. And that alone is far too coincidental to be a coincidence … right? I mean, I suppose it's possible, in a "anything is possible" kind of way. But there is something familiar about her, too. I think I've seen her face before, but I haven't read any of her books. Maybe I saw something online about her? Perhaps an article about one of her books.

Miller and I are becoming quite serious. Soon, it will be a year together.

Diary, I'm thinking about leaving Adam. It feels so good to finally admit that! To get it out.

In the past, my affairs have been merely a tool—an act of rebellion during my search for freedom and a distraction from my very real fear of aging. Adam was even a part of that: get married, have the babies, buy the apartment. It all fit as nicely as puzzle pieces … living the life we're 'supposed' to live in order to be a "normal" part of the human race.

Miller is different. Miller and I are different.

I know he has a wife.

That's the only problem.

And when you have a problem, you have to get rid of it.

Kill it. By any means necessary.

Maureen

xx

#11

I don't have time for pleasantries anymore, diary. We're old friends now, anyway.

I knew there was something familiar about Diana Steinbeck … and she IS Miller's wife! I just about fainted when it all came crashing down during our last session.

Jealousy and raged coursed through my body; I nearly wanted to explode, a thousand embers igniting inside of me like something from an incinerator when she said, "Miller wasn't there!" during our last session. I knew right away when she said his name that she was referring to Miller Steinbeck. My Miller Steinbeck. Mine. Mine. Mine.

I admit, I felt awful hearing about her sad home life. And I do feel guilty about taking what's truly not mine when I have a husband and two children at home. AM I selfish? In some ways, she is everything I'm not.

Imagine my surprise seeing her in our apartment just the other night for a dinner Adam arranged. When I walked in and saw her on the couch braiding my daughter's hair, I felt something sinister flood through me. I don't think she's evil, or even a bad person, honestly … but something tells me she knows a lot more about Miller and me than she's letting on.

Something about the nature of how we met doesn't add up. She's a writer doing research. Yet when I see her take notes, she doesn't seem to be capturing what I say. She either can process information quicker than a starving mouse in a cheese factory, or it's all a farce.

I wonder, what else is she lying about? I mean, she spins lies for a living. Does she live a lie, as well?

I have to keep myself safe. I have to protect myself and my family … and Miller.

Maureen

xx

#12

Everything started here, and now, it all must end here.

Miller ended things with me. He chose Diana.

I begged and begged. I lost my mind, threatened him with a knife, with suicide. His response? "See a therapist! Get over it!" And then, like garbage, he tossed me out, yelling, "What kind of mother, what kind of wife, cheats on her life? You're just an ungrateful bitch!"

Could he be right?

I thought about every word he said on my way home, openly crying as I walked the streets without a care in the world as to who might see me.

I'm not a good woman. I'm not a good mother. I'm not a good wife. I'm not a good therapist.

I don't deserve to live.

I'm sorry to say that this is it, diary. This is our farewell. And not just ours—yours and mine—but mine to the world.

Since it was in this journal that I captured the beginning of the end, it only seems fitting for it to be where I leave my note. That's right. By the time anyone finds this, I'll be long gone. I can't do this anymore.

This is for my family:

I am sorry I have to leave you this way.

I have done some very terrible things I'm ashamed to admit here, but just know that in doing this to myself, some justice will be served. Life will be better without me in it.

To my husband: thank you for the life you have helped me live, and for our daughters.

To my girls, Jane and Eloise: Mummy loves you. I have always loved you and will always love you. You are my reason for having stayed as long as I have. I will not allow you to carry the weight of my sins. So I will wash them away, and drown in them.

I hope one day, you can forgive me.

Maureen Sinclair

xx

I put the diary down, run into the nearest bathroom, across the hall from Diana's office, and vomit.

CHAPTER TWENTY
MAUREEN

I'm sick for at least ten minutes, well aware of my vulnerability if Miller were to arrive back … if Diana were to unexpectedly return.

After the initial shock wears off, I flush the toilet, wipe around the rim, and spray some air freshener I find in a wicker basket on the countertop to eliminate any evidence of my bile. Still sitting on the floor, I prop myself up against the wall, hand on the edge of the closed lid, trying to process what I just read.

Diana Steinbeck's manifesto, of sorts, about me.

What does she plan on doing with it … with these writings? She has me *committing suicide* at the end!

It isn't fiction. It isn't psychology related.

It's murder. It's … revenge. *Vengeance.*

"I'd like to break down a bit of the psychology of venge-

ance," Diana said during a recent session.

"Okay. Revenge." I hadn't given much thought to swapping out the word, but Diana was adamant about it.

"Vengeance*,"* she'd repeated. Purposefully. "Do you think there are any cases in which vengeance is appropriate?"

I must have validated it as an emotion—because it is. The desire for revenge, *vengeance,* and in some cases, restitution, is completely natural. Even expected. There are several traumas that warrant this feeling, so long as there is no violence against one's self or another. In fact, I'm sure I *did* validate that emotion. And she had clarified: "so long as it isn't murder, in real life."

I'm starting to understand—I was right in my initial judgement, however unorthodox for someone in my position: Diana *wasn't* seeking me out for my expertise and research purposes.

There isn't a book. There never was a book.

The awkward topic changes and sporadic questions, some that didn't seem to sync with others, now make sense. She was making them up as she went along.

My anxiety festers into anger. She played the part well. She used me. Humiliated me.

She did the same when she attended the dinner party … when she had my daughter—my flesh and blood—on her lap, hair intertwined in her fingers as she braided it … when she was *touching my child.*

Now I wonder … is Miller in on it, too?

There are so many lies and inaccuracies in those diary entries: how I feel about Diana, parts of how Miller and I met, and the development of our relationship.

But there are also truths.

And that is what frightens me the most.

My previous affairs (which I haven't told Miller about) and the feelings I had after giving birth to my daughters: trapped, questioning my love and attraction to Adam, why I got married and had children in the first place.

Diana is an author. She can conjure up stories to create a fictitious life, romance, death, and make it realistic. She knows how to outline the perfect couple, portray a devious affair, and use it to her advantage.

That isn't even what I'm upset about—well, not entirely—but the *details* of my affair and my daughters' lives. How could she know about that?

Adam.

He's the only one who knows about my affair … but even he doesn't know *all* the details.

Suddenly, there is a bang at the front door, and I hear Miller yell.

The chain lock. Shit.

"One second!" I force my still-in-shock, tense, aching

body off the floor and scurry to the front door. I slow down as I reach it, feeling both lightheaded and anxious. "Sorry," I say as I push the door closed, look through the peephole, unhook the chain, and open it for Miller.

"What the fuck? What are you doing?" Miller glances around the apartment like he's scanning it to see if I have stolen anything, or if anyone else is inside. He looks back at me, down on me, waiting for me to say something.

"Sorry, really. I just felt creepy standing in your apartment when your wife could come in at any moment. I guess I just didn't want her barging in and finding me."

"I told you, she's …"

"I know what you said, but you never know … things come up. Would you want to come home and find another man, one that was fucking your wife, standing in your living room?"

"I guess not," he says with a deep sigh. I notice the Duane Reade bag at his side, with the pregnancy tests inside.

"So, you got them?" I ask. He nods. "What took you so long?"

"I had to walk down a couple of blocks. The Walgreens on the corner is closed, and I didn't want to chance being spotted."

"By Diana?"

He shrugs, like he doesn't want to admit he also has his

own suspicions and worries.

"Well, shall I?"

"Yeah. I guess. Why don't you use the master bath? Just in case..." *Diana comes in, is what he wants to say, but doesn't.* "Do you have to pee? I can get you some iced tea ..."

I shake my head. In fact, I really do have to pee. Another sure sign of pregnancy.

I take the bag and hand him the receipt, reminding him to throw it out.

He nods and crumples it, putting it in his pants pocket.

I walk down the hall into his bedroom, *their bedroom,* and then into the master bath. I close the door and unbox each pre-gnancy test. I have a total of six. The number seems exce-ssive, but better safe than sorry, I suppose. I peel off my pants and underwear, grab a stick, hold it between my legs, and wait. I get a little stage fright before I release myself.

I repeat this process four times, four sticks, before I am completely empty.

I lay them out on the counter and wait the necessary couple of minutes.

As I wash my hands, I stare back at my reflection in the mirror. I am tired of *feeling* reflective. Like I am merely a mirror to everyone else.

A knock on the door startles me. "You done?" Miller asks.

Annoyed by feeling rushed, I open it and nod. I have no

words for him; the tests will speak for me.

He stands over me and waits for the two pink lines to appear, which they do. "Shit," he says. He fluffs his hair, keeping his hand on the back of his neck as he looks down. "I'm sorry."

"Sorry?" I ask. He nods. "For?"

"Well, I'm equally responsible," he admits.

"Thank you," I say. Any fear of Miller being involved in Diana's scheme—whatever it may be—dissipates. There is genuine compassion in his words and posture. His face hangs, and his mouth is closed in a thin line.

"I thought you're on the pill," he says.

"I am, Miller, but things happen. I don't know." He scoffs, and it sets me off. "What is your fucking problem?" I'm shouting, now. I don't mean to, but it feels like an appropriate release of emotions, considering everything I'm dealing with. It's liberating, and necessary. "I haven't forced you into anything!" I pause, and think of Diana … of the diary, journal, manifesto in her office. "This is just as much your responsibility as it is mine!"

"Didn't I just say that?" he says. *Another scoff.*

"There! Right there! That *scoff*." I mimic it.

"I just …"

I don't say anything. I give him the time and space to collect himself, to find the words, knowing when you assume you know what someone wants to say, or how they want to say it, *their* version of words or events becomes distorted, figuratively speaking. I don't want anything that I say to deter Miller from his own thoughts and opinions.

"I was going to end things. Between us. Today."

"Was?"

"Am. I *am* ending things between us," he says. Posture taller, confident, hands in his pockets.

"Still? *Even now?*"

He nods. "Yes. Even now."

"You sure you want to do that?"

CHAPTER TWENTY-ONE
DIANA

I hadn't quite put together that, in order for me to actually get away with the murder of Maureen Sinclair, I would have to write *The Wife I Should Be.*

After all, I can't very well claim to have been meeting with her for research for a book I never wrote.

And this all occurred to me last night around midnight.

Miller is a heavy sleeper, so slipping out of bed and into my office to officially draft the novel wasn't difficult. I had spent so much time trying to avoid the book I am not writing while writing Maureen's suicide diary that I had forgotten this key part of my alibi, should I need one.

Somehow, I managed to compile about sixty-thousand words for Sam. Not quite long enough yet, but that's okay. I have some of the actual notes I did take during my sessions with Maureen—I couldn't very well spend the entire time writing about her. She isn't that interesting, anyway. And they were helpful enough to inspire about two-hundred pages.

I always carry a draft of my novel in a brown leather-bound binder, so when I walk into Tessa, a Mediterranean restaurant on the Upper West Side where I am meeting Sam at the bar, his face lights up as he notices it clutched at my side.

He stands and embraces me before pulling a chair out for me. "First drink's on me!"

"How about all drinks on you?" I laugh.

"Actually, all drinks should be on you." He rubs his thumb against his middle and index finger, making the money gesture.

I chuckle. "Touché."

We order our usual: Sam, a scotch, neat; me, vodka with soda and lime. "You sure you don't want anything to eat?" he asks.

"I'm meeting Miller after this, but thanks."

Miller—my thoughts immediately go to him and Maureen at the apartment. I wonder how it's going.

He nods, tilting his head thoughtfully to the side. Not like he doesn't believe me entirely, but like he has some doubts.

I place a hand over his. "I promise." For a while, my friends knew not to ask me about food, whether I'm hungry or not, as it often acted as a trigger … the weight of a heavy reminder. "Plus, it looks like you're going to be doing some cooking later?" I gesture toward the Citarella bag by his feet.

He nods. "Okay, so let me see the book!" He holds his hands out as if preparing to hold a newborn baby.

When the drinks arrive, I squeeze the lime into the glass and pace my drinking as Sam reads through the first couple of pages. And another few after that. And another few after that.

As self-conscious as I am about a book I technically have no plans on publishing, I'm eager to hear his thoughts. I haven't written in a very long time, so I did have fun "free writing," as I call it. I didn't do an outline, at least not more than a page's worth; I wrote it mostly on a whim. Still, I'm curious about how he finds it.

Maybe, somehow, I would publish it after all.

"Well, whatya think?" I ask, still nursing my drink.

He looks at me, first with a slightly confused expression followed by a smile. He takes a small sip and releases an "ah" as he swallows. "Diana, this is incredible. Rarely have I seen a first draft this good."

I can't help but nod my head two or three times in an aggressive manner, like I can't believe what I'd just heard. "*What?*"

"I'm serious. Eden is such a compelling and colorful character, despite her, well …"

"Capacity for murder?" I ask.

"Yes, and that's just it … you totally get her and kind of love her for it."

"For killing?"

"No, for the psychology of *why* she's a murderer. You *get* it. I have read a lot of mysteries, horrors, and psychological thrillers, and you've really got something with this one." He opens to the first page and reads the first line out loud: "'The decision to kill your husband is not an easy one to make.' I mean, damn."

I cringe, but shake it off with a smile.

Sam wouldn't just say that. He knows how to critique my work when he feels something isn't working or if a piece needs to be re-worked or re-written entirely. So, when he says this, I nod and say, "Well, thank you. That's shocking to hear, seeing as …" I take a sip of my drink, unable to form the words.

"Seeing as?"

"Seeing as this is my 'come-back' book," I say, using air quotes.

"You didn't go anywhere. You're still here."

I smile like he's right, but know he's wrong.

"I really think with some more detail like you indicated you were going to add in some areas, we aren't that far away from editing and publishing," he continues.

I realize now that I can use Sam's eagerness and loyalty to

both our professional relationship and friendship to my advantage here. I don't want anything to seem out of the ordinary, just in case something does get traced back to me. So, I had to put together something for him—and for myself—should I need it. After all, when Dr. Maureen Sinclair is murdered, if the cops suspect any foul play, I don't know if they would talk with her patients. I don't know if doctor-patient confidentiality extends to after a therapist dies … or if after a patient dies, for that matter. When it comes to a suspected murder, I assume the police won't care much about violations of ethics, if it means holding someone's killer accountable and getting justice for the victim.

But between Maureen and myself, *who is the real victim, and who is the real perpetrator?*

When Maureen does turn up dead, I need a solid story to back me up … which is exactly why I spent most of the weekend writing up a very long and lengthy draft of *The Wife I Should Be.*

I smile. "You think so?" I ask Sam.

CHAPTER TWENTY-TWO
DIANA

The rest of my meeting with Sam is a blur. I was only half paying attention. I feel guilty about lying to him. Maybe publishing the novel, after all, will erase some of that. The truth is, I've gotten so good at lying, even I don't know what's true anymore. I no longer recognize myself, or know why I've come to *this* as my only option.

Miller and I meet at Serafina as planned. He is sitting in a booth near the back, nursing a club soda when I embrace him from behind. Wrapping my arms around his warm neck, I breathe in the scent of his eucalyptus shampoo, still lingering on the strands of his hair. "You're here early," he says.

"You too, huh?"

He turns and looks at the partially empty restaurant. "They sat me early. How's Sam?"

"Good," I say, without offering any more detail.

"Just 'good'?"

"He loves my manuscript," I share in a low, humble whisper.

He takes my hand and rubs it, kisses it, and tells me how great that is. How happy I should be, and how happy he is to see me back to my *old self.* "Sorry, I didn't mean it like that," he says immediately, squeezing my hand. "I meant, back to writing. It's the real love of your life." He smiles.

"One of them," I return the squeeze.

He's silent as the *awareness* of Maureen Sinclair lingers in the air between us. We say nothing until the waiter comes over, takes our drink orders (two waters), and leaves.

"So," I say, "How did it go?"

"She's crazy."

I feel the blood rushing to my ears, instantly angry. "*Crazy*," I repeat. "It's so easy for people to manipulate and hurt others and then just label them as crazy."

"She wouldn't accept it," is all Miller says. He drums his fingers around the rim of the glass of water, condensation dripping down the side onto the white tablecloth.

I inhale sharply, keeping myself from saying anything I know I shouldn't. Instead, I ask, "Are we not going to talk about the Sinclairs?"

His mouth slowly falls open into a small o shape; his pupils dilate. "What do you mean?" he asks, trying to play off his obvious nerves.

"The dinner."

"What about it?"

"Maureen. Maureen Sinclair."

"When did you … how did y–"

"It's been a while, Mil. I don't want to go into all of it right now, but I saw the two of you out together. I can't tell you how much that hurt me, Miller. Seeing you with another woman … knowing you were with another woman *again*. How much pain that caused me. I'm a writer, and yet there is no language I can find to describe it."

"Diana, I–"

"No, Miller. No."

He looks uncomfortable. After a moment, he says, "She isn't going to go easily. I've tried before."

"I'm not sure I can do this anymore. I've thought long and hard, for years, about the kind of wife and woman you deserve to come home to. The respect, love, communication, care, and appreciation. But I have realized that I deserve that, too. I deserve the very same things I've been working so hard to give you. I don't know how I could have been so blind. I don't know why I have put all of the pressure of our relationship on myself. There's more to a relationship than fertility, though I understand it plays a huge part in it."

"I–"

"But the idea of you making love to another woman … possibly *confiding* in another woman … I deserve better than that, Miller." Tears stream down my face. I didn't even realize it, until our waiter comes over, shoots me an apologetic smile, and backs away. "I deserve better than trying to surprise you at work and seeing your face light up at a woman who isn't me on the first day I'm even able to leave the apartment since losing Marnie. I do."

Miller says nothing. I watch as tears fill his eyes, too, but then I look away. This isn't about his grief. It's about mine. I reach for the linen napkin and dab under my eyes, my cheeks, even my chin. I pull my hair back into a tight ponytail and take a sip of water, trying to get my nervous system to relax.

"She's pregnant." I say it as a statement. I don't ask. I know.

Miller isn't good at hiding his emotions, and they are instantly revealed on his face, like splashes of color. "Isn't she?" I follow up when he lets too much time pass in silence.

"She just told me this after–"

"And?"

"Diana. It's still you. It's always …"

I want to leave. Find someone else; someone who can give you everything you want, the child you want. I want to go because I want you to be happy.

Those are the words that spilled out of me when I was lost

in vast depths of pain after we lost Marnie. When he tried to console me, I had pushed him away, not wanting him to see how broken I was on the inside. I was afraid he would see me as nothing. But he didn't. He saw me for me.

Now, with the reality of Maureen hanging between us, the truth about what she can give him—what *any* fertile and (somewhat) beautiful woman could—scares me. "Miller, stop. Just …" My head feels like it might explode. I'm craving another drink … the kind I know once I start, I won't be able to stop.

My dependency on alcohol is no different than my dependency on pills, except that the pills were easier, more manageable. Drinking was easier to wean off of; it didn't feel like *weaning* at all, really. I had cut down to once a week or so with dinner.

But now, I need one.

"I want you to be there for that kid," I say. "But I can't be involved. Not in any way. Even with you."

"She's not even sure she wants to keep it."

Another look surely reveals my renewed anger. He immediately starts apologizing, and while it hurts, I say, "Every woman is entitled to her own … doing." It's hard to say, to agree with the words, but it's the only way I see out of the conversation I don't want to have. In many ways, I'm sick of talking about babies, pregnancy, fertility. How can you move forward when you're stuck in the past?

"And next time I decide I'm not ready to accept a gift–" I point to my engagement ring, hoping he will make the connection as to what I'm about to say– "you may want to give me a little more time than a few days before you go off and give it to her."

The following nights, Miller sleeps on the couch. We don't speak; I have nothing to say, and I assume he doesn't, either. The last few weeks felt like we had finally rekindled and worked out some issues. No more. It was all squandered. And I hate that it's because of Maureen. I'd hate it being because of any woman, really. If Miller and I are going to separate, having it be on our own accord would be preferable.

I cancel my weekly meeting with Maureen. I'm still anxious about cancelling entirely, given my plan and Miller's involvement with her, should my sessions become evident to the police. I tell her I have a family emergency, before quickly realizing I'd already told her I wasn't close with my family, and that Miller is all I have.

But what she thinks doesn't matter. The ball is in my court.

I know she's aware that I know about her affair with my husband. I hope the diary she read in my office was enough. I'd left it carefully out for her to find, knowing she wouldn't do anything about it. Her affair is a liability to her.

Still, any assumptions she has gathered are two-fold.

One week from today, Maureen Sinclair will be dead.

CHAPTER TWENTY-THREE MAUREEN

I thought Miller and I could come to some sort of agreement about the pregnancy. But nearly a week after storming out of his apartment and completely forgetting about the cryptic manifesto in Diana Steinbeck's office, I am still at a loss.

Diana cancelled today's session, claiming she has to deal with a family emergency. I wonder if she knows I found out about her plan, in that little notebook. I also wonder if Miller told her about the pregnancy, and whether that news will spare me or hasten that plan.

Still, the question remains about what to do.

"Thanks for meeting me," I tell Miller, sitting at the table in Luke's apartment. "Thank you for hearing me out. This is your baby, too, and I know you're probably not going to want to hear this, but I need you. *We* need you."

He doesn't say much at first … just sits with his hands

crossed over his knee, leaning back in his chair. He dressed light: a black button-up top, trench coat, gray jeans, and loafers. He twiddles with his wedding ring, spinning it around his finger with his thumb. Perhaps unconsciously, but given his composure, it feels deliberate. I can't discern the look on his face. Was it ... *sympathy*?

I flash back to something he once told me following an argument he had with Diana:

"After the first couple of miscarriages, I started to be okay with the notion of being childless. I would've been happy with one, maybe a few years after we were married. But then it became an obsession with her. Like my dick was only a tool. It turned me off."

"You felt used?"

He laughed, smugly. "She can use my dick as a tool as much as she wants, really. What do I care? The more for me, the better. But when she failed, she made it seem like I failed." He scoffed and gestured down at his pants. "I did my part."

"Did she fail?"

"At what?"

I shrugged. "At anything."

He looked out into the darkening city sky. It was past two in the morning, and more and more of the yellow dots in sq-

uare windows faded to black. Following a gentle sigh, he said, "In some ways, yes."

It was the only time I ever heard him speak of her so harshly. Now, looking at the man sitting before me, I wonder … had he been lying, then? Telling me what he thought I wanted to hear, to get what he wanted?

Guilt slithers up my spine like a snake.

More questions tumble through my mind as I stare at him. Had Diana *really* let him down? Or were his accusations a reflection of his own grandiosity, self-arrogance, and unfulfillment? Indulging my fantasy world where we are married, would I actually be left at home with the baby while he's deep into another woman, talking about how *I* failed him too?

Would I let him down? Probably.

I catch Miller's eye and smile out of obligation.

"I thought you were getting an abortion," he says flatly. "It's your body, your choice … but I thought that was the plan."

"It's like you said: *was*. It *was* the plan. It isn't any longer."

Anger flashes in his eyes.

"You're a crazy bitch. Do you know that?!" His entire demeanor shifts. He's practically oozing from the mouth.

I lift an eyebrow. "A crazy bitch you know you're in love

with."

He looks at me, incredulous.

"You can't leave me," I calmly continue. "You said you love me, too …"

This seems to bring him down a level, and his eyes soften slightly. I see my Miller there.

"I was wrong for that, and–"

"Please, don't leave me, Miller. You can't. Don't leave *us*. I'm not happy with Adam. I want you. I can make you happier than–"

"This isn't about happiness," he says calmly. "It's about … convenience."

Convenience.

I don't think twice before slapping him across the face. Nearly feeling the pain myself, I wipe the tears streaming down my cheeks, embarrassed and hurt.

"You can't do this. You can't. I swear I will kill myself!"

I don't believe what I'm saying—I blame the hormones—as I remember Diana's plan. I don't dare say anything to Miller about it.

"Maureen, stop!" Miller kneels before me, grabbing a hold of my arms while I break down, and in a whisper, he says, "What is the matter with you? Are you crazy? You're a therapist, for crying out loud!" I hide my face with my palms. "I'm sorry, Maureen. But this is the way it has to be. *I love my wife.*"

"But what about *me*?!" I break free from his grip. "You said you loved me! You *asked* if I ever thought about being your wife!"

"When did I say that?" he asks, incredulous.

"A couple of weeks ago!"

"Lower your voice," he commands. "I don't want the neighbors to hear you and call the cops."

"I don't care who hears me! You told me you wanted me to be your wife when I asked you about her name. You said, 'Do you want it to be yours?'"

Now, it's his turn to bury his face in his hands. Whether he is ashamed or just frustrated, I can't tell. "I'm sorry you took it that way, but that was …"

"A lie?"

"Foreplay."

I can't control my anger any longer. I hit his chest with my fists, shouting, "So, a lie!"

"No. Not a lie, Maureen!" He pushes me away from him, holding me back with one arm.

"It was *not* just foreplay. Don't manipulate it. It's exactly what it sounded like … romance, love! And stop calling me Maureen!" I stand, shouting again. "Call me 'Ree,' 'baby,' 'Maur' … anything but Maureen!"

"But that *is* your name. And who's manipulating who

now? I've said a lot of romantic things, but it doesn't mean …"

Everything is spiraling out of control.

"It doesn't mean you're in love with me?" I finish for him.

For what feels like several minutes, he says nothing, though I know it's only one or two. "Where is this coming from all of the sudden? Maybe it's just pregnancy hormones, emotions. I thought we both knew it was never for the long haul."

"I guess I've changed," I say, forcing myself to calm down.

Miller's eyes meet mine, and for a moment, I think there could still be hope. I am sure I see a glimpse of the warmth I am used to there.

But then, he speaks.

"I'm sorry, Maureen. But I haven't. My wife and I have been working on reconnecting lately, and I've been trying to sort out my own feelings here. Yes, I feel love for you, in some ways. I also know I've disrespected my wife, and I'm a douche. A total dick. But I feel things, too." Here, his gaze noticeably shifts to my belly. "Look, I'm responsible for this, too," he finally says after a few minutes. His voice is gentle, sad. "If you want to keep this baby, I won't abandon him. He deserves a father."

I don't know the sex of the baby, but Miller giving it an identity makes the experience feel even more real. Hope surges through me again.

"But I need you to understand, Maureen … I don't love you the way I love my wife. I don't know if we will come out of this or not, but I have to give us the chance. And not while I'm cheating on her with you. It won't be honest that way."

"How is it honest now?" I can barely choke the words out.

"It isn't," he says. "And that's why I have to end it. Like I said, my feelings for you were something I needed to sort out, but the pregnancy, well … it scares me, Maureen. It really does. Not in a new parent kind of way, but in a …"

"'I don't want to be with you' kind of way," I finish for him.

The rejection is so painful, it drains my energy. I am completely worn out.

He nods. "I'm sorry."

"No, you're not. People who actually feel remorse do something about it." I can't look at him … can hardly speak.

"What would you like me to do?"

"Be there for me during this pregnancy." It's barely more than a whisper.

"Maureen, I just told you we have to end our affair."

The silence hangs in the air for several moments. I'm not sure what is happening inside me, but finally, an eerie sense of calm settles over me.

"Everything will change when he's born. He'll remember he loves me."

Miller visibly startles, and the movement reminds me he's here. *Did I say it out loud?*

"You need help, Maureen. You threatened to kill yourself. Twice. Threatened to hurt the baby if I didn't come here, and now–"

There is an instead break in the fog in my mind. "What? I never threatened to hurt the baby if you didn't come here."

"When you texted me."

"I didn't. I called you to ask you to come here this morning. I don't know what you're–" before I can finish, he's turn-ing his phone over to me, displaying our text messages.

And there it is, surrounded by a gray bubble: Miller. Meet me tonight, same place, or I'll hurt myself AND the baby. Please. I'm begging you to hear me out.

I force myself to my feet and rush to my phone, scrolling to find my stream with Miller.

Miller. Meet me tonight, same place, or I'll hurt myself AND the baby. Please. I'm begging you to hear me out.

But *I know* I didn't send it.

CHAPTER TWENTY-FOUR
DIANA

Brooklyn is far.

At least, Coney Island is. The ride out feels never-ending.

I don't want to kill Maureen out of spite of her pregnancy. But I *am* going to kill her out of spite.

When I wrote out my plans, I thought of it as an outline for my next book. When I began executing it, I never let it get too personal; I didn't invest time into learning the personal side of Maureen's life or family. Only what I needed for the diary.

It's perhaps a cliché, the diary. Stories of her affair as a crutch for her unescapable end. Then again, some of the best stories, best life lessons, are clichés. The platitudes we tell ourselves and each other.

Everything I shared with her about my struggling marriage and infertility was meticulously calculated, and all the information I received from her was extracted without emotion—clinically and scientifically.

If I allowed myself to see Maureen Sinclair as a human being, I wouldn't be able to carry out my plan. I am not cold or heartless. I simply believe in justice. And sometimes, you have to transform a belief into an action. One thing I have learned over the last few years is that we *do* have control over ourselves. Even over the uncontrollable.

On a fertility forum, I once read the following: *We can try surrogacy and IVF, and we can most certainly adopt. We have choices to have a child. Whether the pain of not giving birth to that child is there or not, we do have opportunity. It's about the actions we take to make what we want happen.*

It's about the actions we take to make what we want happen.

The diary is the key to making Maureen's death look like a suicide. Writing it wasn't easy, both in terms of content and matching her handwriting. Stealing some of the handwritten notes from her office when she was in the restroom. "Go on and head in, I'll be right there," she'd say.

Then came the storyline … I began the process the same way I do all my novels; I had to think of Maureen and Miller, create a storyline for them, some good and some bad, and make her look like an obsessed, love-bombing girlfriend who, after getting turned down, can't live with herself. So, she takes her own life.

I don't want Miller connected to Maureen's death. Despite how much he might deserve it.

There is a possibility, though, that if her death is considered suspicious or due to foul play, they will investigate every inch of her life. They will look into her work and personal life, and Miller will most likely come up. An extramarital lover would shoot straight to the top of the list of suspects, alongside her husband.

Protecting Miller is the last thing I will do as his wife, before I do, inevitably, leave him. It is a decision I never expected to come to at the end of all this. In fact, this was supposed to *save* us. But if love—trust, connection, communication—alone cannot protect or repair a couple, this certainly won't, either.

I start crying, feeling the pain of the loss of my marriage heavy in my chest at this realization and consequent acceptance. It will take time to heal.

The diary has to make Miller look like a good guy. An unhappily married man seeking out sex and only sex so, if questioned, his answers match up.

But the pregnancy makes things more complicated. The leading cause of death of pregnant women in this country is violence by a partner … which includes an unhappily married man seeking out sex and only sex. Right?

I can almost taste the salt in the air when I step off the train at Coney Island. The beach is deserted, as I gaze out at it.

"You're late," comes a voice from behind me.

"Relax. I'm on time."

"Not late in time. Late in payback."

I laugh as I take Robert Merrill's hand and descend down the stairs.

CHAPTER TWENTY-FIVE
MAUREEN

Naturally, I would be more afraid to leave the apartment at four o'clock in the morning and disappear into the New York night without my husband by my side.

Adam woke me hastily, saying something about an emergency. Thankfully, our kind, 70-year-old neighbor just down the hall, Mrs. Alethia, was able to come stay in the apartment while our daughters sleep.

Forget autumn, *winter* is definitely in the air; I can barely move without my teeth chattering as Adam guides me out of the apartment building and into the parking garage in the basement, his hand under my forearm.

"What happened? Why won't you tell me what's going on? Where are we going that we need to *drive*?" We never drive in Manhattan, as it's nearly impossible to navigate the overcrowded streets anymore, let alone find parking. Aside from the handful of times we pack up the car and head out to Long Island or spend the day in Brooklyn—Prospect Park, the botanical gardens, Dumbo—or drive up to Yonkers to grocery shop at Stew Leonards and Costco.

Being in the best shape of his life, Adam's heavy breaths are an obvious result of his nervousness around this "emergency"—whatever it is that forced us out of bed and to wherever we're going. "It isn't far," he says without looking at me. "But we can't walk there. Please don't ask questions—we have to hurry!"

When we reach our apparent destination—which is *not* a hospital or hotel or airport or any place that would make rushing out in the early morning hours justifiable, but a corner block on the South and Clinton Street off the East River—Adam exits the car and comes around to open my door. Still searching his face for answers, I let him take my hand as I, too, step out into the night.

There, standing in a long, black, wool trench coat, jeans, and high black boots is Diana Steinbeck.

And she's smiling.

"Wh-what are you doing here?" I turn to look at Adam again, but he won't look at me. He's staring at Diana, who doesn't answer my question, smiling too.

The smile never leaves her face.

Diana knows I already know.

CHAPTER TWENTY-SIX MAUREEN

"I found the diary," I say, my voice shaking. The fear is becoming a living thing inside me, and I have to break the silence. "I know everything."

Diana chuckles and shakes her head. She doesn't seem surprised. In fact, she seems very sure of herself, as if this is exactly how things should be.

She laughs, a sort of cackle laugh. "You really think I'd leave something like that just lying around if I didn't *want* you to find it?" She shakes her head.

Feeling embarrassed, but still determine to spare myself, my baby growing inside of me, my life, I ask, "How did you know I would?"

"Are you *that* delusional?" She shakes her head again, like I should have figured this part out. "You think Miller would actually bring you into our apartment on his own?" Her grin makes me more uncomfortable than her previous, devilish smile. "*We* planned it that way. Miller and me. Well, just the part where you come to the apartment. I knew you'd snoop around. That's the kind of person you are. Trying so hard to find a slice of life in a crumbling marriage that you took part in destroying. Of course, I couldn't be sure that you would go into my office and prowl through my stuff, but it brings me satisfaction knowing you did exactly what I thought you would."

"I was a puppet in this show," I confirm.

"Exactly."

"So, he did know?" It was all I could think about, Miller's part in it.

"Miller knows nothing," she says. Then she looks down at her hand and laugh, "Do men ever?" she asks. Talking to me as if we are having drinks at the bar, engaging in some girl talk.

"I don't follow," I admit.

"I've known about the affair for a long time, but it wasn't until recently that I told Miller," Diana began. "I wanted to work on our marriage—this isn't his first affair, you know. I understood his need to for affection and connection, given how much I have changed over the past few years. He was, is, someone who lies and cheats, and essentially, so am I. Just in a different way. So, I asked him to meet you at our apartment, counting on you to be skeevy enough to snoop around … to learn more about the woman whose husband you're fucking."

I bite the inside of my cheek at the word. I am completely and unequivocally shameful. For everything I have done and everything I am. I stand before Diana warmly dressed, bundled up, but naked. The emperor with no clothes. She continues, seemingly utterly unbothered by the cold wind. The air around us is quiet; the city that never sleeps is somehow tucked away in slumber. There is abandoned construction to our right and two tents for, what I assume, the homeless. The only break in silence is the occasional squawks of the pigeons that fly and land around us.

"And so, there's no book?" I ask.

"Oh, oh there's a book. There will be one," she nods assuring. I'll need some sort of proof that my work with you, at least my seeing you, was legitimate, should it ever come to that."

"But why? Why all this? Why go through months of those sessions, getting close to me…"

"I wanted to watch you squirm. I wanted you to know that I know," Diana says, devoid of emotion.

"Why?"

She smiles. "To get you here. Now."

The pieces begin clicking together. No, she surely couldn't. A hurt woman is very different than an actual psychopath … "You're not really going to kill me, are you?" I ask, half-joking. Thinking it isn't real. It can't be. *This*, here and now, is when I die. My mind won't allow me to think otherwise.

Diana leans back, shifting all her weight onto her back foot, digging around in her purse while scanning me up and down. Ignoring my question, she finally says, "Why you? The fuck is so special about you?" Her voice reveals her disgust. She abandons her search and slowly approaches me, flicking my hair over my shoulder. "Receding, like an old man's. Gray. Flat." She walks around me, an entire three-hundred-and-sixty degrees. "I would say your body is unflattering, but you did have two children. I won't insult their existence by what it did to your body." She pauses. "Anyway, I'm sure you despise it enough as is. Though I'm sure he made you feel really good about it, didn't he?" The last sentence, she whispers in my ear.

When she pulls away from me, I see the anger all over her face. I have no response. I deserve every hateful word.

"I guess you're at least somewhat intelligent, being a 'doctor,' or whatever the fuck it is you label yourself. I don't really give a shit. But recite to me a line from William Faulkner, or better yet, name one thing he's written."

I stand silently, still trembling from the cold, fidgeting in place like an impatient child waiting to get into an amusement park. I can't control it. The cold has seeped through my clothes and into my bones.

"I didn't think so," Diana continues. "You will never, ever know him like I do. You might be the woman he strung along to fuck, but I'm the woman he doesn't want to leave."

Her voice cracks at that, despite the grin on her face.

"Diana, I know how you must be feeling …"

"You have no idea what I feel."

"No. You're right. But I can empathize with the emotions …"

"Oh, Maureen. Fucking enough. You really talk too much."

"You have every right to *want* to do whatever it is you plan to do to me. But Diana … you're not a murderer …"

"Of course she is," a voice says out of nowhere.

Suddenly, I see a figure emerge from behind Diana, like a very carefully executed cinematic sequence in an Alfred Hitchcock film. And I'm afraid I know exactly what body will match the slate silhouette.

CHAPTER TWENTY-SEVEN
DIANA

It is taking more out of me than I can describe to have this confrontation with Maureen. Other, ethical, therapists might consider it therapeutic, though perhaps not in the way I'm doing it. Regardless, saying all the things I've been wanting to for so long to Maureen *is* liberating.

The look on her face as Robert takes his place next to me is one I wish I could photograph, frame, and include in a first-edition copy of *The Wife I Should Be* for my enjoyment only.

Robert Merrill and I met when I was doing research at the hospital for *The Convent.* At the time, he was a patient.

In addition to the group therapy sessions I observed, I worked closely with some of the patients in in-patient care. With signed waivers, I was able to sit in on a few sessions and talk with them.

Robert confided in me about a relationship he'd had with

'someone of a higher power'... someone who had been entrusted with helping him. This person played a pretty major role in his psychotic break. Months after *The Convent* was released, I received a letter from Robert about how much he loved the book.

I hadn't heard from him again, until several months ago, when I rather serendipitously, it seems, ran into him.

In New York, you never run into the people you hope to—an ex or friend. It's the most random people, like your gynecologist, picking out her fruits and vegetables right next to you at Gristedes—(yes, that really happened).

When I saw Robert emerging from the Q Train in Chinatown, we got to talking, and then went for coffee.

He seemed well, rehabilitated.

Then, he told me, in greater detail, of what really happened that drove him to institutionalization.

I told him I believed his story; call me naive, but some stories are so intricately shared that only a true psychopath—or perhaps a writer, like myself—could dish out the lies so precisely *and* recount it exactly the same each time. Even I need outlines to remind me. Something in his tone told me he was sincere.

"Maureen Sinclair," he disclosed just weeks after finding out Miller had been sleeping with a "Dr. Maureen Sinclair."

I knew about the ways in which he had hurt Maureen—the

oral rape while holding her hostage in her office—so I was sure to keep my distance. I don't condone his actions, but I also know how it feels to have an out-of-body experience … to feel like you are going crazy. I had many of them after my miscarriages.

I listened to Robert talk, and out of my own utter disbelief, frustration, and *need* to tell *someone*, I confessed that she—"his" Maureen—was having an affair with my husband.

Robert's shock was evident on his face. Once he recovered, he simply asked, "And you're going to let her get away with it?"

I wasn't sure what I was going to do. But it certainly wasn't going to be nothing.

Almost one year later, I stand before Dr. Maureen Sinclair, whose expression screams, *please … have mercy on me.*

CHAPTER TWENTY-EIGHT
MAUREEN

When I see Robert, I am transported back to when he was in my office, attacking me, and I freeze. Seeing Robert is far more frightening than anything I read in the diary. I know what he is capable of. I have already lived it.

But how do they…

"Maureen, Robert; Robert, Maureen," Diana says. "Though you two already know each other."

I look back at Adam, who still won't look me in the eye, but he looks confused, like he didn't know he was part of the plan.

"Adam…please," I plead.

He still says, still does, nothing.

I turn my attention back to Diana and Robert. "Please … don't hurt me. Whatever it is you want, I'll do it. *Please*."

"Relax, Maureen," Diana says. "Enough of the waterworks."

I turn to face Robert, a flash of anger coursing through me. "You told her things I only told you." I look to Diana, referencing the diary, and say, "that's how you got the details."

"Some of them," she admits.

"You didn't want me to tell the police, or any of my doctors, the truth about what you did to me, did you? I owe you nothing." The hatred in Robert's voice was ominous. "In fact, you owe me," he says.

"What *we* did to *each other*," I couldn't help but say.

"Oh, shut the fuck up," Diana says. "You were his *doctor*." She practically spits the words at me.

"It's okay, Diana," Robert says. "I'm well over it."

"And yet you're standing here before me now," I throw back.

"I saw an opportunity," Diana says, redirecting my attention to her. "See, my plan was simple: frighten you a bit, make you think you were going crazy thinking someone is following you, and write the diary entries—your story. Whether or not all of it is 'true' doesn't really matter. I just needed enough for the police to corroborate your death as a suicide after finding it in your office." She stops, pulls the notebook out of her jacket, and waves it in the air at me. "You asked me if I'm really going to kill you. The answer is no. I'm not going to kill you. Though I admit, I was fully planning to."

"*You're not*?" Robert asks in utter disbelief. Diana doesn't answer him, keeping her attention firmly fixed on me. "Diana!" he shouts. She shakes her head, refusing to look at him.

"You crazy bitch," he says. "I'm not getting caught here, doing, whatever this is then. I'm not getting sent back," was all he said before he hurried off. Diana not looking as her accomplice picked up speed, jogging away.

Adam doesn't look either, but I swear I sense some guilt on his face.

I burst into tears, unable to control them any longer. Though I had felt sure she wasn't capable of killing me at first, the tension had risen to the point of creating a very real fear for my life. Now, with my face in my hands, I thank Diana for her mercy.

"You're right. I am better than a murderer," Diana says as her face slightly softens. "We live in the memory of the people we love. I may not have a child, but I am a mother, and what I planned to do is not going to be the legacy I leave for myself or my name." She stops, openly scoffing as she looks me up and down again.

She walks closer, each menacing step making me more and more uncomfortable until she is so close to my face, I can practically feel her breath on my nose. "You aren't worth it …" Her words are slow and deliberate. Then, she tears her eyes away from mine to focus on something behind me. Again, her cold, haunting grin sends shivers down my spine as she backs away from me.

Instinctually, I turn to look behind me, at Adam.

And instead of the relief I know I should feel, there is only terror.

CHAPTER TWENTY-NINE
MAUREEN

I have just about eight rocks comfortably tucked into the pockets of my sundress. It's not all black, like the kind you would typically find on a New York woman. It's a very pale yellow, not quite pastel. A soft crème, really. Small sun-flowers with tiny red buds in the middle bleed through from top to bottom. The dress hangs nearly down to my ankles, which are covered by heavy leather boots with a small heel. I'd have said "chunky," but that word disgusts me. *Chunky, moist, and flow*: three words that should be struck from the dictionary.

Anyway, back to the rocks. There are four in each pocket, each nearly palm-size. Some are wet—a soft gray, with dark patches from the moisture—and some are dry. They are heavy, their surfaces fuzzy, like thick dust coating a smooth surface, and some feel a rigid.

The rocks weigh me down, pulling on the dress and causing it to hang low on me. *The point of the rocks.*

But I did not put them there. *Another point of the rocks.*

It is interesting—the ways in which the mind blocks out trauma. How my brain is focused on the kind of dress I am wearing and the size and texture of the rocks, instead of the fact that they are weighing me down in the East River.

Adam is finally looking me right in the eyes for the first time all night. He is carrying me in his arms to the water, and neither of us are able to look away.

When he has waded out far enough for the water to touch my skin, he ever so slowly begins lowering me in. I am half-way beneath the water's surface when I come to understand that he is enjoying every moment of what he is doing.

I beg for my life and that of my unborn child. "Please wait a few months … until …" I can't go on.

He is unaffected. Calm.

"You really thought I didn't know?" he asks when he finally speaks. He holds me carefully, making sure my head is the only thing left above the surface of the water, so I can hear him. "Do you give any of the people in your life any credit? Of course, I knew, Maureen. I always knew. I saw the messages, and the satisfied look on your face when you arrived home, time and time again. And I saw how your body was changing. I watched you during two pregnancies … I *knew.*

"I sent that text to Miller, begging him to meet you. I'd

hoped you would do something about it, the affair, *the baby*, but being the narcissist, you are, of course you didn't. Did you?"

"You two were always in it together?" I ask him. "Showing up at my apartment and all?"

Diana, beside him, says, "No. It really was a coincidence. We ran into each other, he invited Miller and myself."

Before she can continue, Adam interrupts her. "I could tell by the look on her face, the lonely, sad, and painful look on her face whenever you and that guy—" he can't even say Miller's name, "looked at each other."

"He called me the next day," Diana admits. "And I told him."

"And so you … you agreed to *this*?" I ask Adam.

He shakes his head. "She was having doubts."

"I told you, I'm better than killing you … myself," Diana calls out from the shoreline. "But watching you take your final breath … I'm not above that, at all."

I stare into Adam's eyes as I feel a single tear slip from my eyes that won't blink. I could swear I could hear Diana laughing.

Adam gently removes his hand from beneath my head and whispers, as I sink lower, "You made me do this. You made me kill you."

November 20th, 2022

NEW YORK, NY – On November 11th, a body was discovered in the East River. Today, she was identified as Dr. Maureen Sinclair, psychologist.

Her husband, Adam Sinclair, feared the worst after finding a suicide note, rather a whole diary, days after the body of Mrs. Sinclair was found, and they pleaded to the public for help. "My wife often left for short trips as an act of selfcare," Mr. Sinclair stated, as to why he did not report her missing earlier.

Mrs. Sinclair was born and raised in the English countryside. She moved to New York City to pursue a doctorate in neuroscience and clinical psychology. She leaves behind her loving husband and two young daughters.

"As a therapist myself, I understand the suffering my wife must have gone through in her final moments," Mr. Sinclair said. "My only solace is in knowing her suffering is over. For all of us."

Acknowledgements

Writing and publishing one book is an incredible and surreal accomplishment, but writing and publishing *a second one* is a dream. Even though it is my career, it never feels like work, and I am so grateful to be a part of this fulfilling field. I would not have the opportunity to do what I love (create, write, and publish stories) without my readers, and the support of those close to me. My parents, Michelle Relyea and James Relyea; John Suarez—*I feel like I've done this before*; Mike Stafford, a profound friend and mentor since the beginning; my editor, Megan Yacovich, who patiently takes in all drafts of my work and sees the masterpiece long before I do. My best girlfriends: Nakira Pauson, Lindsey Salute, Nicole and Natalie Perez, and Marisol Manica—the first person I shared this story with (on a ten-minute voice note)—for your support and love; my professors from college, Alexandra Shelley and Joe Salvatore of The New School, and teachers in high school for their invaluable encouragement and support; and, of course, Lisa—whose support and guidance restored my light.

A PREVIEW OF ALLISON'S NEXT BOOK,
MURDER WITHIN THE PAGES,
COMING SPRING 2025

PART ONE

A word is dead
When it is said,
Some say.
I say it just
Begins to live
That day.

—Emily Dickinson

NOW

June 7th 2024

CHAPTER ONE

My mother died when I was eleven years old.

Taken, murdered.

The last gift my mother ever gave me was a collection of poetry by Emily Dickinson. It was a rare edition she found in a local bookshop in London. Palm sized, it was thick and black; with gold quilling along the front, and bleeding into the spine, it weaved along the book like ivy on a gothic, metal gate leading to an enchanted (or disenchanted) mansion. The title simply read *Selected Poems by Emily Dickinson.* On the bottom back, it said, Notting Hill Press.

The day after my mother gave it to me, lines underlined and annotated, filled with her thoughts, she was never seen again.

During Mom's flight back from London, she annotated the book for me. She highlighted stanzas she said reminded her of me, some she thought I could relate to, and her favorites. Som-ething she often did when she gifted me a book. She wrote comments like, *this reminds me of how I felt the day you were born*, or *you will grow up and unveil feelings of what [Albert] Camus has written here*, or *be not afraid of life, but inspired by it.*

"Natty," she once said, "literature, and all forms of writing, are some of the most important things we will ever have as humans. The capability and capacity to not only identify what we are feeling or experiencing, but to have the courage to write it down and share it."

She wanted me to be educated. To know not just about literature and writers from Shakespeare to current day authors, but politics, science, psychology, art, and finance too. "I don't care what side of politics you're on," she once said, "only that you pick a side, and know what you are talking about; what is happening in the world and what it means."

The police ruled her dead based on the length of time she had been missing, her wallet and phone found safely in her purse at home, suspected by a serial killer had been targeting women, more specifically mothers. He was dubbed the *Massachusetts Masochist*. They believed she fit his modus operandi, his pattern.

My copy of *Selected Poems by Emily Dickinson* disappeared that day as well.

In some way, her notes in there were her final words to me.

The police botched her investigation. I know they did. There was a lack of evidence to prove she was one of the victims of the Massachusetts Masochist. I think differently.

And with a gun to my head, something in my gut tells me I am right.

By Allison Relyea

Fiction:

You Made Me Kill You

A Cure Through Love

Poetic Self-Help:

Undoing Unearthing Becoming

The Honeymoon of Healing

medicine

Allison Relyea is an author born and raised in New York City. She graduated from The New School with a degree in creative writing. She is the author of two psychological thrillers, A Cure Through Love and You Made Me Kill You, and three poetic self-help books: medicine, The Honeymoon of Healing, and Undoing Unearthing and Becoming. Combining her love of storytelling and real-world experiences, Allison sets to entertain and support readers along the way. She lives in Arizona.

Instagram: @allisonrelyeawriter
TikTok: @allison.writes
allisonrelyeawriter.com

Printed in Great Britain
by Amazon